SILKEN TREMORS
SYBIL LeGRAND

**A
SECOND CHANCE AT LOVE
BOOK**

To Becky at Georgetown:
may this book have helped her in her quest
for the Golden Slipper that will
get her presented at the Court of St. James,
with only a few Ouagadougous
and Tegucigalpas on the way.

And to Mary Anne and her Derek.

CHAPTER ONE

"HI! THIS IS Sidney McKenna. I'm not available at the moment, but please leave your name and number when this thing goes 'beep,' and I'll get back to you as soon as possible." There followed a sound more like a squawk than a beep, and another voice said, "Sidney, this is Jock. I've got a hot one for you. Real foot in the door, if you can make it. Mr. Chips himself. Can you get to my office by four today?"

Sidney let the answering-machine tape run for a few more moments. There were no other messages of importance, only Brice's plaintive cry, left twice: "Sidney, don't you *ever* stay home?"

She checked her watch. It was two-thirty and she began calculating backward from four o'clock. Could she make it to Jock's office? Her car was in the shop, so that meant the bus, and the bus meant forty-five minutes. Make that an hour to get there, which meant she'd have to leave by three. And that meant she had half an hour to change clothes and put away the two bags of groceries sitting on the kitchen table. She'd lugged them up the hill, which meant she needed a shower, too. Also, her two cats had escaped out the back door earlier, and it would take at least ten minutes to corral them. No way could she make it to Jock's by four. Whoever Mr. Chips was, no matter how important he was, he'd just have to wait for another time.

Jock was a good friend. He tried to throw business Sidney's way, but sometimes he was just a bit overenthusiastic. Like the time he'd gotten her a client who needed a translation from Maltese. Now, that had been a real foot in the door, she thought. Twenty-seven phone calls to find the only person in San Francisco who spoke Maltese, to translate two paragraphs. With her luck, Mr. Chips—what a weird name—was into Urdu or Kurdish.

An ominous wetness was beginning to appear at the bottom of the brown paper grocery bags, which meant that her frozen food was beginning to thaw. Sighing, she unhooked the answering machine, took off her parka, and began putting the groceries away. Having no car was a real pain. Before, she'd been able to go shopping once a week, but now, since she could carry only two bags, she had to go three times as often, and that seemed to be mostly for cat food. What sane person had two cats, anyway? She slammed a can of soup into a cupboard with a loud clunk and then heard a familiar precise voice:

"My, my, aren't we letting it all hang out today?"

Brice Lorraine, the very definition of tall, dark, and handsome, was leaning on the frame of her open back door. He was Sidney's next-door neighbor, who lived in a Victorian cottage identical with hers in everything but the paint job. She was used to his habit of wandering into her house unannounced, but this day, the timing was wrong.

"Why aren't you at work?" she snapped, pulling a smashed loaf of bread out of the bag. Typical, she thought—always put the bread under the cans.

Brice drawled, "Took the afternoon off. I've got a friend coming over and I'm fixing a fantastic dinner. That's why I'm here."

"To invite me?" Sidney said suspiciously.

"No. Safeway's out of artichoke hearts. You got any?"

"No!" Sidney picked up the remaining full bag to move

it to the more convenient counter, and the wet bottom ripped out, littering the floor with cat-food cans, packages of frozen vegetables, bath soap, and several pounds of hamburger.

"Oh, damn it all!" Sidney said, and sat down as cans rolled every which way across the floor. She kicked a package of frozen broccoli across the room to Brice. "Here, use this. And shut the door. You born in a barn or something?"

Brice leaned down in his lanky graceful way and scooped up the broccoli. "Not a bad idea. Might even work," he said, closing the door and sitting down opposite her across the butcher-block table.

Sidney attacked. "You're a big help! You borrow my food when I have to carry it up here, you clog up my answering machine with dumb messages, and now you just sit there and watch the cat food roll around." She glared at him.

"Always did hate manual labor," Brice said with a yawn, "but here, if it makes you feel better..." He picked up a single can of cat food and put it on the table.

"Brice! My God! I just thought of something!" she said, sitting bolt upright in her chair. "What does 'Mr. Chips' mean to you?"

Brice did not seem at all startled by this sudden digression. "Ummmm," he said, looking studiously at the ceiling. "Is there a prize?"

"I'm serious."

"Oh, okay. Mr. Chips. A book. A movie. Peter O'Toole. English schoolteacher. How'm I doing?"

"Not so good. Think Silicon Valley."

"Oh, *that* Mr. Chips. Yeah, he owns Pacific Instruments, down in Sunnyvale. The bank has loaned him some money, I think."

"But what's his real name, Brice?"

"Damned if I know. I remember the headlines when his wife walked out on him and took half his corporation with her. The gossip columns loved it. 'Good-bye, Mr. Chips.'"

"But you're sure it's Pacific Instruments? *The* Pacific Instruments?"

"I'm positive."

Sidney leaped up. "I've got to get out of here. Jock was right. This *is* the big one. I'm going to break into Silicon Valley." She looked at the kitchen clock. "Egad, I've got twenty minutes to get to the bus stop. Help!"

Thank heavens for Brice, she thought as she showered. Through the water's blast she could hear him putting away the groceries and retrieving the cats. As she worried about what to wear, he yelled through the door, "The Evan Picone—the banker's suit. That'll impress 'em." So she put on the black pinstripe, with the vest, and a man-tailored white shirt, with only a hint of lace at the collar and cuffs to relieve the severity. She peered into the mirror myopically, cursing under her breath at the dilemma of people who wore glasses and had to put eye makeup on. Brice was right, she should have gotten contact lenses instead of that stained-glass window for her house.

She could see at a distance well enough, but close up was a problem. She still had trouble getting mascara on the long lashes over the clear blue eyes that peered blurrily back at her. She made a few stabs at it. At least the black brows like two wings above her eyes didn't need any help, nor did the pink and white skin over the small straight nose or the "interesting" (as Brice termed them) cheeks and chin. But the hair did. Black and curling, it was constantly out of control because of rain in the winter and fog in the summer. She couldn't win. She'd finally settled on pulling it back into some version of a French twist, but tendrils were still flying around her face when she'd stepped out of the bedroom.

Brice was waiting with her attaché case. Sidney grabbed it. "How do I look? Okay? Are my shoes in there? Bless you for not asking any questions. I'll explain it all when I get back."

She reached up, way up, and planted a kiss in the air next to Brice's black moustache. "Feed my cats. 'Bye."

In exactly the allotted twenty minutes, she was seated on the bus. As it groaned and chugged along, she ignored the gloomy fog outside that obscured the streets, and checked her attaché case. Business cards, brochures, blank contracts,

calculator. Good. All there. Glasses. Glasses. Not there.
The little case was empty. Well, she'd wing it. At least her
black pumps were in the case. She mustn't forget to take
off her blue-and-white Nikes when she got into Jock's office
building. She'd already guessed that her jogging shoes and
banker's suit were the reason for the stares of the plump
lady in the raincoat in the seat behind the driver. Well, lady,
she thought, you try running downhill three blocks in high
heels sometime. Everyone's wearing Nikes downtown anyway.

While the lady continued to stare, Sidney thought about
the job she hoped to get that afternoon. It really could be
her big break. Money and stardom. Or at least enough
money to fix the Volkswagen bug and the roof on the house.
Buy contacts, even. She'd been hoping to get a client from
Silicon Valley for several years. Her business ran on referrals, and all she needed was one job from which she
could leapfrog to another and another. And Silicon Valley
was *the* place, and Pacific Instruments was in the heart of
it.

"California Street. Cable car for Nob Hill, Chinatown,
Market Street," called out the bus driver for the benefit of
the tourists on the bus. Sidney fumbled for her transfer and
followed the crush through the back door. For once, there
was a cable car waiting—which meant that she'd be almost
on time. She climbed aboard, taking an inside seat—the
tourists always got the outside ones. The gripman, in his
beret, rang a predictable "shave and a haircut" on the bell
and pushed on the long lever that connected the car to the
moving cable under the street. There was a jerk, and the
little trolley rocked and creaked slowly up the hill. The
tourists beamed.

"Do you know you're riding a national monument?" said
one man to his small son, both of them bundled to the teeth
in parkas. Sidney noted that there were others clinging to
the outside of the car wearing only T-shirts and shorts. The
inevitable, she thought. They think California summers are
hot. Well, they are, everywhere but on this little foggy
peninsula. Why, even only a few miles away, in places like

Silicon Valley, for instance, it was hot now.

She tried to remember if she'd ever seen the Pacific Instruments buildings in Silicon Valley, but she couldn't. All those electronics firms down there looked alike—long, low buildings with beautiful landscaping that gave them a campuslike atmosphere, everyone said. Only a few years before, Silicon Valley had been called the Santa Clara Valley and was completely planted with orchards. Now it was the eighth wonder of the world, all those booming companies, fueling the world's hunger for computer technology. All of them making zillions of dollars because of a thing the size of her fingernail—the silicon chip. Amazing. And Pacific Instruments was one of the first, and one of the biggest. She *had* to get that job!

Exactly then, the cable car broke out of the fog, just at the top of Nob Hill. Everyone blinked in the bright sunshine, and there was a murmur of *oooh*'s as soaring Grace Cathedral and the elegant old hotels hove into view. The gripman began a more urgent tattoo of warning as the cable car clanked across a busy street and tilted crazily downward. Sidney looked ahead down the long hill, and between the dark canyon walls of the buildings saw the sun sparkling on the bay. Her spirits soared. San Francisco always had this effect on her. No matter how depressed or anxious she was, all she needed to do was go to the top of a hill somewhere in the city, look around, and thank her lucky stars she lived in it. She was the eternal tourist in her own hometown. Suddenly, she knew she was going to get the job. On a day like this, in a place like this, how could she fail?

She shouldered her way off the car at the bottom of the hill and, dodging across the street against the light, ran up the steps of the Bank of America Building. In the wide plaza beside the black stone abstract sculpture called "Banker's Heart" by the locals, she paused to look up at the brown sandstone-and-glass skyscraper towering above. A cloud, scudding along in the sea breeze, appeared from behind the building, and Sidney had the dizzy feeling that the massive building itself was moving.

That reminded her of the elevators—those monstrous

express numbers that flung you up, or dropped you down, fifty floors in a few seconds, leaving your stomach ten floors behind. There was no way around it, though. The law firm that Jock worked for was on one of the highest floors, and she wasn't about to walk, she thought. Gritting her teeth, she dashed into the building and scooted into a red-carpeted elevator just as the doors were closing. The other people in the elevator looked perfectly comfortable and didn't even flinch when the elevator came to its swooping stops.

As she stepped into the plush reception room of Jarndyce, Cooley, and Alexander, Sidney realized that she was now both light-headed and slightly airsick, just from the building. But she smoothed down her Evan Picone uniform nonetheless and marched as professionally as possible across an acre or two of Oriental rug to where a receptionist dressed like a slightly punk fashion model sat behind a desk about half as long as a football field.

"Jock Eddy, please. He's expecting me," Sidney said in her most authoritative voice to the receptionist, who merely raised her thin, plucked eyebrows and stared. Her fingernails were at least an inch long, painted brown and squared off at the tips. After a long silence, the receptionist looked down at a slip of pink paper in front of her and said, in a bored nasal twang:

"Sidney McKenna?"

"Yes," Sidney said, suppressing the urge to say "ma'am," which would reveal that she felt intimidated.

"You may go in," sneered the receptionist.

Irked with herself for feeling gratitude at having received this gracious permission, Sidney stalked down the long hall to Jock's office. Seated in front of it was Jock's own secretary, who, blessedly, recognized Sidney and buzzed Jock on the intercom.

Jock came out to meet her, closing the door behind him. His prematurely silver hair was, as usual, set off by his perfectly tailored gray suit, reminding Sidney that the other lawyers she knew all seemed to have wardrobes made up entirely of rumpled brown off-the-rack suits.

"Come on in," Jock said, putting his arm around Sidney's

shoulder. "You're a little late. You should have called. I was afraid you hadn't checked your answering machine." He pushed her gently toward the door of his office.

"Wait a minute, Jock," Sidney whispered. "What's this all about?"

"He'll explain. Pacific Instruments is going multinational. Lots of tricky translations needed. Right up your alley."

"*Who* will explain? I don't even know this guy's name," Sidney was saying, just as Jock opened the door and she was pushed, reluctant and balky, into the office.

Sitting in one of the deep leather wing chairs opposite Jock's cluttered desk was the most disconcertingly handsome man Sidney had ever seen. His hair was very dark, a little curly, and beautifully cut. His face was hawklike, with a fine line of mouth over perfect white teeth. A deep tan set off his piercing green eyes. He was, Sidney estimated, not yet forty—certainly younger than she'd expected. He reminded her somehow of a pirate.

Then she realized that she was standing stock still, staring at him. And then she further realized that he was staring back, looking her over arrogantly, and grinning a devilish grin—which was why she could see his perfect teeth. Making a distinct effort, Sidney looked back at Jock, who was, to her chagrin, grinning too.

"Sidney McKenna, this is Philip Oliver, chief executive officer of Pacific Instruments," Jock said, and what seemed to be about ten feet of lean body unwound itself from the leather chair and extended a hand. It was then Sidney saw why they were grinning, for Philip Oliver was clad in a black pinstripe suit, just like hers, including the vest. Of course, he didn't have on a skirt, and there wasn't any lace on his collar and cuffs, and he was wearing black shoes instead of . . . blue-and-white Nikes.

"Good of you to come. I know it's hard to get away on Fridays." Philip Oliver's voice was deep and clear, with a trace of an accent that Sidney, even in her flustered state, identified as East Coast—New York, probably. She managed to shuffle halfway across the intervening space to shake his hand. She muttered something she hoped sounded like, "My pleasure," though it certainly wasn't true. She felt a complete fool.

Jock came to the rescue and maneuvered her to a chair identical to the one that Oliver was again seated in. He made a clever lawyerly little speech about how good Sidney was, how many languages she spoke, and how much in demand she was because of her ability and education. Describing her simultaneous translations in the courtroom, he praised her to the skies. Sidney wasn't listening. Jock thought she was wonderful, she knew that, but this disconcerting man was just sitting there looking at her with a faint, cool grin, looking as if he didn't believe a word of it.

When Jock had run down, there was a long silence, as Philip Oliver continued to look at her, but the cool grin had turned to a polite smile of inquiry. Sidney knew this game: the first person to speak was the loser, and though she desperately wanted this job, her prospective employer's facial expressions and everything else about him—including his damn suit—annoyed her. She smiled back, just as politely and just as silently. Jock was looking back and forth at the two of them and must have known full well what was going on—after all, he'd taught her the trick. But he looked now as if he didn't approve.

Finally, Oliver said, "And how did you come to learn so many languages?" in a tone of voice that implied that anyone who looked like she did probably couldn't speak anything at all. Knowing she'd lost, Sidney glanced at Jock, who was now smiling, and swallowed her pride.

"My father was—is—a mining engineer," she said, "and I grew up in Chile and Venezuela, so I learned Spanish. I spoke English at home, took French and Portuguese in school, and learned Cantonese and Mandarin from my Chinese grandmother, who lived with us."

Mr. Chips's eyebrows had gone up at the mention of her Chinese grandmother, as everyone else's always did, and Sidney hoped she wouldn't have to go into that explanation. When he said nothing, she continued:

"I learned to read and write Chinese in college."

"And what college was that?" Oliver asked.

"Berkeley. I majored in Business. I'm working on my M.B.A. now—it's going pretty slowly, though, I'm afraid."

"So you are familiar with finance terms, then?"

"Yes," she said, though the innocuous word *finance* always set up a slight reverberation in her head. Other people reacted to words like *Hawaii* or *moonlight*. She reacted to *finance*. But then, other people, or at least most of them, hadn't once been married to Max the Magician.

"But most of my translation work has been either legal or medical," she added hastily and then wished she hadn't. Never volunteer anything in a job interview, that's what they always said.

"And have you ever interpreted at, say, a business conference?" He was looking at her more closely now, though she could read nothing in his face.

"No, not a business conference. But I can do simultaneous translation in Spanish, French, and Chinese. That means I can be only three words behind the speaker. I'm certified by the State of California." Sidney opened her attaché case, and her black shoes fell out with a clunk. Damn, she thought, stuffing them back in and searching through the papers under them. If only she'd taken time to find her glasses! At last she triumphantly pulled out a brochure and a certificate and handed them to Oliver.

"Here," she said. "You can get my qualifications from these."

He looked at the brochure carefully and then at the certificate.

"Well, I see you were twenty-nine last Thursday, for one thing," he drawled. "And that you were born in San Francisco, at French Hospital. Weighed six pounds, seven—"

Sidney rocketed from her chair, stumbling over her open attaché case, and rudely snatched her birth certificate from his hand. Her face felt hot. She glanced over at Jock, who seemed to be trying very hard not to laugh. She could not look at Philip Oliver.

Studying her feet in their Nikes, she explained, "I lost my driver's license and needed my birth certificate to get a new one. I forgot to put it away. I . . ." She stopped. Why was she being so apologetic? The man undoubtedly thought she was a card-carrying nitwit anyway. The job was almost certainly lost. She looked up, catching, as she'd expected, a glint of humor in his eye.

"Do you have a card?" he said.

Luckily, she kept her cards in her jacket pocket, so she fished one out and handed it to him.

"I'll certainly keep you in mind," he said. "Thanks for your time."

Sidney was, she knew, dismissed. She had expected it anyway, the minute she laid eyes on the man. She snapped her attaché case shut and turned to Jock.

"I'll see you and Dolores at dinner next week," she said. and mustering all her dignity, she left, closing the door smartly behind her. She wouldn't stick around to hear Jock's inevitable critique of her performance. It would only turn into another of his "funny Sidney stories."

She stepped into the elevator, and, as it dropped forty floors she held her hand against her stomach in a futile attempt to hold it in place. She was still clutching her midriff when she emerged onto the street into a milling mob of people pouring out of the Montgomery Street high rises. A crowd of people within the mob stood at the curb peering up the California Street hill—obviously waiting for the cable car. As she made her way across the tracks, she heard the whining rattle of the cable fall silent. That meant the cable car wasn't running and that sooner or later, probably much, much later, the Municipal Railway Company, fondly called the Muni, would send a bus to pick up the unfortunates. The rest of the crowd heard the cable stop, too, for there was a mass groan and everyone began moving out in all directions for alternate routes home.

For Sidney, there was no choice but the long hike to Market Street. Blessing her Nikes, she elbowed her way through the packed sidewalks. But when she got to Market, she saw an enormous traffic jam—not a car or bus was moving on that main artery. A teenager in a Giants jacket, holding a big black box radio—which, thankfully, was not

adding its clamor to the already tumultuous street noises—
had somehow managed to climb one of the ornate Victorian
light poles.

"What's going on?" Sidney yelled up at him: "Can you
see?"

"Yeah, man. It's a big fire. They got hook-and-ladders
all over the place. Must be a five-alarmer." He looked
inordinately pleased. "Market's completely closed." He slid
down the pole, turned up his radio, and sauntered in the
direction of the fire, clearing a path through the annoyed
pedestrians with ear-shattering rock music.

Sidney considered her options. There weren't many. She
could walk out, but all the buses and trolleys were caught
behind the fire trucks. She didn't have enough money for
a cab. Worse yet, she was getting hungry, and a cold wind
was beginning to whistle down the long sweep of Market
from Twin Peaks. She wandered back onto Montgomery,
out of the wind, and her stomach rumbled. She didn't have
enough money to eat down here, either.

Then she remembered Paoli's. Of course. Paoli's was
said to be the last bar in the world that served enough free
hors d'oeuvres to make a meal, and it was only a couple
of blocks down. She could afford to buy the requisite one
drink, entitling her to fill up on free food. After an hour or
three, the traffic would probably have cleared up, and she
could go home.

Evidently, a lot of other people had had the same idea,
for Paoli's was jammed. The piano player was in full swing,
and people were already singing along and shouting re-
quests. She'd never be able to find a seat—but then again,
in that crowd, she probably wouldn't have to buy a drink
either. Clutching her attaché case to her chest, she sidled
through the crowd, toward the food trays. Managing to free
one hand, she started wolfing small pieces of pizza, until a
waitress, easing past holding a tray of drinks high over her
head, glared at her. Apparently, she was being a bit obvious,
Sidney decided, so she took a napkin, piled some stuffed
eggs and slices of spinach quiche on it, one-handed, and
stood in the center of the crowd around the bar, where no

one would notice she didn't have a drink. Snatches of conversation eddied around her.

"So, naturally, the computer was down when they called...."

"... bought a case of Pinot Chardonnay for fifty bucks..."

"... snowed in at Tahoe for a week, and at the wrong end of the lake, too..."

"... third parking ticket this month, and it was in my own driveway..."

"My place or yours?"

"Wells Fargo is closing down their whole division..."

"I said, *my place or yours?*"

Sidney came to with a start, for evidently this last remark was directed at her, and a hand was snaking past her elbow from behind, holding a drink in front of her.

Mortally offended at this classic pick-up line, Sidney wheeled as best she could, considering that her attaché case was between her feet and her hands were full of deviled eggs, and said, as coolly as possible:

"I beg your pardon?"

Mr. Chips was towering over her, looking at her with that same amused grin. "I saw you sneaking the food, and thought you might need a drink before they caught on. I've got a table over there, if you'd care to join me." He cocked his head toward the piano. "Or you can drink it here, if you like."

If Sidney had earlier felt like a complete fool in front of this man, she could not find a word in her vocabulary for her present feelings.

She stood in her jogging shoes, her hands full of filched food, and glared in defensive outrage. She looked at those perfect teeth and wondered if they were capped. Too bad there wasn't a piece of spinach from the quiche stuck between the two front ones. He probably flossed ten minutes a night anyway. Mr. Perfect. He probably...

"I realize that's a difficult decision to make on the spur of the moment," he was saying. He looked down at her feet. "But if you'd like to jog over, I'll carry your drink."

He walked away, and she followed, suddenly deflated. What did she care? She'd already bombed out on the job, and it would be nice to sit down. And a drink did sound good.

The seats he'd found were simply two chairs crowded up to a packed round table. The crowd was getting very mellow, and the piano player had broken into "San Francisco." The people at the table were all clapping rhythmically and bellowing, "San Francisco, la da di da di da," for everyone knew the tune, but not the words. Squeezing herself into a chair between Philip Oliver and a prematurely bald young man in a tight tan three-piece suit, who was slapping his stubby hand, with its prominently displayed class ring, on the table in time to the music, Sidney shouted:

"I can't get a bus."

"What?" Philip Oliver shouted back.

The song wound down, to scattered applause, followed by one of those sudden inexplicable silences that occasionally falls over an entire roomful of people, and into that silence Sidney heard herself yelling:

"I mean, I don't usually come to places like this."

Every head in the room swiveled in her direction, and there were shouts of "Sure, baby" and "We've heard that one before." The piano player said into the microphone bent over the keyboard, "For the lady in the pinstripe suit, an old Duke Ellington favorite," and began to play "Don't Get Around Much Anymore."

I'm dreaming this, Sidney thought. Why didn't I stay home and put the groceries away? Why didn't I walk home? Why don't I just go and jump off the bridge? She sat and looked down at her lap. Gradually the piano segued into something else and the talk around her rose to normal decibel levels. Then she felt something resting on her arm and saw it was a lean brown hand with a white cuff and black pinstripe sleeve attached. Philip Oliver leaned over and said in her ear:

"Is your luck always this bad?" and there was real sympathy in his voice—or perhaps it was pity.

She nodded glumly. "I can't get home because the Muni's

not moving, my car's in the shop and I haven't got the money to get it out, my roof leaks, the bottom of my grocery bag broke, I forgot my glasses, I forgot to change my shoes, I'm wearing this stupid suit, and now that. That's about my usual day."

"I don't think the suit's so stupid," he said, grinning piratically. Or baring his teeth—she couldn't tell.

"See, I've done it again." she said gloomily. "It looks fine on you—just stupid on me. We must look like a tap-dancing team. Ask the piano player to do 'Me and My Shadow,' will you?"

He burst out laughing, a deep, rich, honest laugh.

"Look, I'm stuck, too," he said. "There's no point in even trying to get out of town with that traffic jam out there, and I happen to have reservations at Ernie's at seven. Wouldn't waiting it out at Ernie's be easier than this?"

She looked up suspiciously. Ernie's was one of the poshest restaurants in town. "Nobody just happens to have reservations at Ernie's," she said. "You have to get them way in advance on a Friday."

"And so I did. I've been stood up. I was going to cancel, but we might as well use them." He looked slightly pained, and Sidney realized she'd put her foot in it again.

"Well," she said contritely, "if you're willing to risk it, I am."

"Risk it?"

"With my luck today, who knows what will happen. I can curdle hollandaise, turn Cabernet Sauvignon into Ripple . . ."

"I can't imagine anything more interesting. Like having dinner with a poltergeist." He laughed.

The din was rising again, so they finished their drinks in silence. Hers, she realized, was Scotch and water. At least he hadn't assumed she drank tacky stuff like piña coladas. The crowd was tuning up on another song, "New York, New York," which a smaller group in a corner was trying to drown out with "Chicago."

Philip Oliver leaned over again and said, "Ready? Let's get out of here before the natives get any more restless."

They struggled out to the street, still jammed with cars, most with their engines turned off and their drivers sitting stonily behind the steering wheels. But pedestrian traffic at least had lightened. They trudged back up Montgomery Street, past the looming dark banks and over the still-silent cable-car tracks. Jaywalking, they crossed the street toward Ernie's elegant maroon awning. As they stepped under it, Oliver put out a hand to stop Sidney.

"You might want to change your shoes before we go in. I don't mind, but that man over there is looking at you funny." He nodded at the doorman in resplendent uniform, who was simultaneously trying to whistle down a taxi and stare at Sidney's feet.

"But if I change, how will they tell us apart?" she said, but she opened her attaché case anyway and pulled out her shoes. Under the watchful eye of the doorman and the curious stares of passers-by, she changed her shoes. Oliver balanced her by holding her elbow as she teetered first on one foot and then the other. His touch gave her the strangest little tingle, somewhere in the vicinity of her diaphragm. How odd, she thought. A little like the Bank of America elevators.

They were early, but the maître d' was most helpful when he heard the name Philip Oliver, and he led them to a corner booth at once. He took Sidney's attaché case to the checkroom for her, and there was an immediate flurry of waiters and wine stewards at the table. Sidney couldn't see to read the menu, so she let Philip do the ordering.

While he chose beef Wellington and picked out a wine from the three-inch-thick leather-bound wine list, Sidney looked around the opulent, red-plush-filled restaurant. A somewhat different feeling hit the pit of her stomach as she located the table where she and Max had sat five years ago, the last time she'd been here. She wondered if Max came here anymore, when he was in town. She discovered that she no longer felt a pang when she thought of Max. Perhaps she could stop avoiding his former hangouts.

"Looking for somebody?" Oliver's voice broke into her thoughts.

"No, not really," she said. "Do you come here often?" she added, to change the subject.

"No, hardly ever," he said flatly.

"But the maître d' jumped through hoops when he heard your name," she objected.

His face darkened and he snapped, "It's my wife's—my ex-wife's—name that he knows, not mine. Mrs. Philip Oliver."

"Oh," was all she could say. Fortunately, a waiter arrived with the pâté and another with the wine, and Philip Oliver was diverted by the mandatory rigmarole of inspecting, uncorking, tasting, and approving. She devoted her attention to the pâté. How did she manage to hit on his sore points like that? But how could she have known?

He broke the long silence by saying, "Okay, tell me all about it."

She looked up, puzzled, scanning his face. He didn't look angry anymore, just pleasant, but she couldn't imagine what he was talking about.

"Your Chinese grandmother, what else?" He was grinning now, and she had to admit the smile was dazzling—and the teeth weren't capped. "You look like an Irish girl, straight from the Old Sod."

"It's a long story," her standard answer slipped out before she could stop it, but she quickly softened it by adding, "but a romantic one. My grandfather, on my mother's side, *was* Irish, or of Irish descent—he was born in San Francisco. He was engineer on a ship—a freighter, I think it was. His ship was docked in Canton, and he happened to meet a beautiful Chinese girl in a park and fell in love with her at first sight. Her family was a very modern one, for those days, and she had a Western education in a convent school. But they wouldn't let her have anything to do with an American."

Philip Oliver was looking at her with interest. The thought crossed her mind that he had the greenest eyes she'd ever seen. They had a compelling gleam. His eyebrows could only be described as rakish, and his—

"You were saying?"

Sidney almost jumped. What on earth was she doing, losing her train of thought like that?

"Well, anyway, she ran away with him. He jumped ship and they went to Rangoon, where mixed marriages weren't so scandalous. My mother was born there. My grandfather brought his wife and daughter back to San Francisco after a few years. He was afraid of what his own family would think—Chinese weren't so welcome here then, either. But they loved her. My mother and father grew up next door to each other—and he was Irish on both sides. So I'm three-quarters Irish and one-quarter Chinese—just like San Francisco."

He smiled. "True, if you ignore the Italians, the Russians, the French, the Koreans, the Mexicans, and so on, but I see what you mean. So you were born here, but lived most of your life in South America?"

"I lived here until I was four, and then my father started working in Chile, and then Caracas. Now my parents are in Peru. We always came back here on home leave, though, so I always thought of it as home. When the time came for me to go to college, I returned here and stayed with my paternal grandparents while attending Berkeley."

"And have stayed here ever since, right?"

"Right."

The beef Wellington was brought to the table with great flourish at that moment, and had to be carved and served. Sidney was glad for the diversion of attention, as the conversation seemed to be heading toward touchy ground. He might ask her why she'd stayed in San Francisco, which would get them into the subject of Max. And Max represented a five-year hiatus in her life she didn't feel like bridging at this moment. Ex-spouses were clearly a no-no at this table anyway.

On the grounds that the best defense was a good offense, she sipped her wine and changed the subject.

"And what about you? Where are you from?"

"New York City. My father was in publishing. He was amazed to have a son who liked engineering." He smiled.

He looked very boyish and appealing when he smiled, she thought.

"Why did you come to California?" she continued.

"My roommate at M.I.T. was out here, doing some graduate work at Stanford. He had some ideas about starting a business, and he knew I had some ideas about semiconductors. I was working for one of those electronics firms outside of Boston, and I really hated working for somebody else. So I borrowed ten grand from my father, moved out here, and my friend and I started a shoestring operation down in Sunnyvale. We had a lot of luck. Plus a good climate, top-notch engineers coming out of Stanford and Berkeley, and research facilities. A typical Silicon Valley story, I guess."

Sidney knew he was right. It *was* a fairly typical story. Youngish millionaires abounded in Silicon Valley. And that recalled to her mind the lost job. Perhaps it wasn't really lost. Perhaps she ought to make another try for it. The wine and the food might be mellowing him, making him forget her unfortunate behavior in Jock's office. She decided to risk it.

"So why are you looking for a translator?" she ventured.

His eyes became hooded and blank. "That's something I'd prefer not to discuss."

Sidney rushed heedlessly on. "But I can guess. You've run into Japanese competition and you're thinking of opening an assembly plant in another country where labor costs are cheaper—probably in Latin America or Asia. Right?" She smiled proudly, knowing from her reading of business publications that she was bang on. All she'd needed was that hint from Jock that Pacific Instruments was going multinational. They'd even discussed a similar case in her Operations Research course.

When he said nothing, she plunged on. "I'm even willing to bet that you're floating a stock issue to finance it."

"So Jock's been talking out of school, has he? I'm surprised." There was cold anger in his eyes now, and his mouth was set in a grim line.

Sidney's heart sank. She'd only been trying to impress him with her intelligence, to parade her knowledge of the business world, but instead, she'd made him think that Jock had revealed privileged information.

"No, no, you've got it all wrong," she protested. "I was just guessing, showing off. Jock never tells me—or anybody else—anything about his work. He knows the rules."

"So does the Securities and Exchange Commission," Oliver said ominously. "Obviously, that was a pretty shrewd guess." He was leaning back in his chair, not eating, looking at her with narrowed eyes.

This was getting worse and worse, she realized. Jock could probably be disbarred.

"Please listen," she begged. "I only put two and two together. I'm getting my M.B.A. and I read the *Wall Street Journal,* and I know that all the companies in Silicon Valley are feeling the competition from the Japanese. A lot of them are opening foreign assembly plants. I speak Chinese and Spanish, and since you considered using me, I figured you were looking at Taiwan or Hong Kong and Latin America, where labor is cheaper. You need money to open a plant." She was talking desperately now, and very fast. "Jock specializes in legal work involving floating stock issues. So I guessed. Honestly, it was just a dumb lucky guess." She pushed her hair back from her face, which felt hot with the effort of trying to convince him of her sincerity.

He continued to look at her long and hard, and then relaxed, a least a little. He picked up his fork again, and said, "I suppose I have to believe you, if only because I can't imagine Jock talking about a stock issue."

Relieved, Sidney began pushing green beans around her plate. Perhaps she owed him more of an explanation. And considering that he was buying her this elegant dinner, a full confession was probably warranted. She no longer wanted the job anyway . . . did she?

"I was trying to prove to you how smart I was, I guess. Hoping you'd reconsider and give me a chance at that job. I thought I'd appeared pretty unprofessional in Jock's office and was trying to make up for it. It was a dumb thing to do, and I'm sorry. It's none of my business. I don't know anything about your company, except that you make silicon chips, and that's only because they call you Mr. Chips."

As soon as the words were out of her mouth, she was ready to go under the table. She had a terrible feeling she knew what was coming.

"There are several reasons why I didn't hire you, and you've just hit on one of them," Philip Oliver said, looking right through her. "I do not appreciate that nickname, and the fact that you knew it is just one more indication that you aren't the person I need for a job as delicate as this one. That and your clothes, and hanging out in Paoli's, and wearing Nikes because all the career women here do it— and your M.B.A., too. It's all part of the San Francisco scene.

"This is a very, very small town," he continued. "Everybody knows everyone else. Especially in the financial district. One little rumor, one piece of inside information dropped in Paoli's or Ernie's, and you can raise or depress a stock value—or ruin a deal. And I'm talking millions of dollars. If this were New York, it wouldn't make much difference, but out here in Lotus Land, everyone is in the same hot tub, exchanging confidences. I can't afford to hire anyone from that crowd. I think you can understand why." He said this in ice-cold tones that reminded Sidney of her father when she had done something especially disappointing to him. Suddenly, her embarrassment dropped away and was replaced by anger.

Oliver, however, evidently noticed nothing, because his expression softened. "Now, why don't we forget about all that, and the job, and enjoy the dinner."

But Sidney was really angry now. First he misunderstood her, then he insulted her, and now he was patronizing her. She put down her fork neatly, placed her hands on the table, and leaned forward, eyes flashing.

"I am *not* part of that crowd," she said softly but distinctly. "They aren't even San Franciscans. They're all from Chicago or New York, pretending to be San Franciscans. Don't you dare categorize me with them. For instance, I

never wear this damn suit, only when I'm down here trying
to impress some big shot from Silicon Valley, and that
happens about once a century."

She paused and took a deep breath.

"And, just for your information, I don't jog in the
Marina—these shoes are for running for buses. I don't live
in a houseboat in Sausalito or a condo on Telegraph Hill.
I don't put down cases of wine in my broom closet. And I
don't go to Paoli's or Perry's or Henry Africa's."

He was looking at her with a smile she would describe
as "tolerant." It only goaded her on.

"In fact, Immigration pulled my green card—I'm an
illegal alien down here. Ask that receptionist at Jock's firm.
She knows. She's the border patrol. She knew I didn't
belong in the financial district. I'll bet she reported me.
You can expect a raid in here any minute. They'll take me
down to Market Street and put me on the first bus headed
west."

Sidney smoothed the napkin in her lap and picked up her
fork.

"And now, if you don't mind, I will finish my dinner
before they get here. And furthermore, I wouldn't have
wanted to work for anyone like you anyway."

She was breathless, but hungry. She tore into the beef
Wellington, feeling much much better. Though the job was
long gone, she'd had the chance of a lifetime, ticking off
this, this . . . New York know-it-all . . . this supercilious silicon snob, this Cupertino calculator contractor . . .

Odd sounds were coming from across the table, and she
hoped he was strangling on his beef Wellington. When he
fell out of his chair, she'd step over his dead body, saying,
"Ta ta, old boy. That's what happens to outsiders here.
They choke on their own words."

But when she looked up, he was sipping his wine, looking
unperturbed.

CHAPTER TWO

SUNDAY MORNING, SIDNEY and Brice were sprawled on her old couch, the Sunday papers strewn around them. On the coffee table were coffee mugs and a bag of doughnuts. It was later than usual, for there had been an argument about whose turn it was to go over to Winchell's for the doughnuts and who was to go to the corner store, Monty's, for the paper. Monty's was closer, but it was uphill.

Sidney had finally gotten out of her bathrobe, thrown on a pair of faded jeans and her red-and-gold San Francisco 49ers sweat shirt, which she'd bought in a moment of fair-weather fanhood a couple of football seasons earlier, and taken things in her own hands by going up for the paper. Sure enough, when she got there, Sam, who had owned Monty's for thirty years, had said, "I thought it was Brice's turn this week." Which was what she'd said all along, she told Brice when she got back. Brice, however, refused to speak further until he'd been through the entire newspaper. He believed it was bad luck to interrupt a Ritual. But Sidney could hardly wait to discuss Mr. Chips—Philip Oliver—with him, so she fidgeted through the comics, the book section, the international news—ugh—and the humor column, before she spoke up.

"Brice, I want to talk about something."

"Shut up," he said amiably. "Can't you see I'm reading?" He put his long, skinny bare feet on the table in front of him, disturbing one of Sidney's cats who was sleeping on the entertainment section.

"Oh, sorry, Harrison," he said politely to the cat, who grumpily sidled past the coffee cups and curled up on the want ads out of range.

Seeing it was hopeless, Sidney started an article in the California Living section about gray whales, but her heart wasn't in it. Brice had gone out somewhere early Saturday morning and hadn't returned till after she'd gone to bed that night. That was the trouble with living in row houses: she'd heard his front door slam, rattling her windows, at midnight. She'd been too tired then to get up.

And she'd needed to talk to him. All day Saturday she had fumed about his defection, while fuming about Philip Oliver in general. It was probably a good thing, come to think of it. She'd spent the day on her hands and knees, muttering to herself and stripping old varnish from the floor in the hall. If she hadn't been mad, she'd never have gotten around to it. She'd been wondering if she'd ever get mad enough to tackle the mess on the shelves in the cellar, but decided that would be carrying things to extremes. But she could see that Brice was starting to come out of his coma, so she snarled at him:

"And were were you all day Saturday, and all night?"

"And where were *you* all afternoon Friday, and all night?" Brice flung back at her.

"I thought you'd never ask," she said. And she told him the whole horrible story, from the opening scene with the Nikes, through the birth certificate, Paoli's, Ernie's and the silent ride home in his BMW or Volvo or Buick or whatever it was.

Brice let her run down, and then said, "But what did he do after you told him you were glad you weren't working for him?"

"Nothing. He didn't even choke, worse luck. We finished eating and he dropped me off at the house on his way home. I don't think he said a word, other than asking directions."

"Damned nice of him, I'd say." Brice stretched and yawned. "He gave you a free dinner and a ride home, and you didn't do a thing for him. You could have thrown in a free translation. Put all his prepositions and conjunctions into Chinese for him, or something."

"Blast you, Brice, will you be serious?" Sidney nearly shrieked. "I've never felt so slandered in my life, and by a paranoid businessman whose parents could afford braces, at that. Or was I out of line? You work with people like that all the time—tell me." She sighed. "Go ahead, what's one more insult. I can handle it."

Brice looked at her with raised eyebrows. "You really mean it? I get a chance to say what I really think without fear of retaliation?" When Sidney merely looked disgustedly at him, he continued, "In that case, I'll give you the benefit of my wisdom. Also some research I did yesterday. I think you really put your foot in it. Aside from the fact that he's right, at least about the atmosphere down on Montgomery Street. You should never talk about anything important down there. It's gossip city."

"Okay, so now I know. Go on." Sidney glowered.

"Well, one of the things I did Saturday was go into the bank to clean up some stuff on my desk. I did some checking while I was there. About a year ago, Pacific Instruments took out a big loan. It's a very good loan for the bank. It's a good company. Low debt ratio and so on."

"So what does that have to do with anything?" Sidney began picking up sections of the paper.

"My guess is that they needed to buy out his wife, who would have been a major shareholder, and who took a walk about then. The company is in a bind now. Sales are down, and they're going to have to go into some other country, where labor costs are lower, to compete with the Japanese. And they need capital for that."

"And they can't borrow any more money, right?"

"Right. Interest rates are too high. No loans, no bonds.

That leaves only equity capital—selling stock to the public. And having to do that is a killer for these entrepreneur types like your Mr. Chips. They're the whiz kids who started a company on a wing and a prayer and an idea, and really flew. Math and engineering is what they know, not business. And once you sell stock, it really isn't your company anymore, even if you retain the majority of the shares. You're still accountable to somebody else, to the stockholders, not to mention the Securities and Exchange Commission. It must be like selling an arm or a leg—a piece of yourself. And you're not the shirt-sleeve boy genius any more, running something on luck and guts and R and D. You're just another middle-aged corporate type. I know, because I do deal with them. Not on the same scale as Mr. Chips, but I'm getting there. So you can figure he's going to be supersensitive about stock issues, among other things. His ego is involved."

Brice got up, stretched, and started a slow meander to the kitchen with his coffee mug. "You'll get all that in M.B.A. 210—Psychology of Management," he said over his shoulder. "I told you to take that instead of Operations Research."

"Yeah, and you told me to wear that damned suit, too, and that caused a lot of trouble." Sidney joined him in the kitchen. Both cats were rubbing up against Brice's Calvin Klein jeans. He got out a can of cat food, opened it, and spooned the food into plastic dishes on the floor beneath the answering machine.

"I fed them already, Brice. They're going to get fat."

"Don't take your human hang-ups out on animals," he replied blandly. "Cats should look like meat loaves."

He opened the back door. "Look, the fog's finally burned off. I was going to go down to the Castro to see what was coming down there, but I think I'll go to the beach instead. Wanna go?"

"No, thanks. I might get a tan, and then everyone would think I was from Peoria or something." Sidney took a deliberate dig at Brice's hometown. "Besides, I want to finish this discussion."

"I thought we *had* finished," Brice complained.

"Was it my fault or his? That I didn't get the job of a lifetime?"

"I'd say both. Just stop fussing about it. The next guy will probably want a klutzy smart-mouth like you. Win a few, lose a few. Write it off to experience. Anyhow, you got a free dinner out of it, didn't you?"

"True, true." Sidney had to agree. She *was* making too much of it. "But why do you suppose he invited me to dinner?"

"Maybe he's got a thing for Nikes."

Brice ambled out the door and climbed over the weatherbeaten wooden fence into his own yard. They could never agree on who actually owned the fence, so no gate had ever been put in, as neither was willing to pay for one. Sidney watched as Brice, a foot taller than she, swung easily over it. She knew what was going to happen. He'd be back in a few hours with the same complaint he registered every time he went to the beach: that he was blue from the cold wind, not tan from the sun. He'd have to wait for his annual vacation, which, being an obsessive-compulsive, although a laid-back one, he always took at the same rented condo on Maui. He came back every year with a gorgeous tan, which then faded in about three days in the fog. Poor Brice.

She put the coffee cups in the sink. Speaking of gorgeous tans, Philip Oliver had one, all right. She wondered where he'd gotten it. Sailing on his yacht? Tennis at the Silverado Country Club? Four minutes a week at a tanning parlor on Folsom Street? Sidney wondered why she had failed to mention his smashing good looks to Brice. Would that have put a different light on her telling of the story?

She headed for the stairs. She had a particularly difficult translation to do this afternoon, one that she had put off far too long. She went into the smaller of the upstairs rooms, the one she'd fitted out with a desk, an old typewriter, a student lamp, and her books. She called it her office—tax-deductible, of course.

Philip Oliver popped back into her mind, unbidden. Write it off to experience, Brice had said. He was right, too, but she still couldn't get that lean face with its crooked grin out of her mind. She knew now that that choking sound she'd heard over the dinner table was laughter. But was it laughter *at* her, or *with* her? Had she been deliberately funny? She couldn't remember. She could only remember being angry.

As well she should be, at herself. A big, beautiful, rich, handsome, tanned, bright, straight single man, and she'd made a fool of herself. But so what? He was way out of her class, so far out of it, in fact, that she couldn't even imagine his lifestyle. Gorgeous women in designer gowns on his arm at the opening of the opera? Lunches at the Captain's Cabin at Trader Vic's? Membership in the Bohemian Club? He probably had a place in Carmel, a flat in London, and a brownstone in New York. Then she remembered he'd been stood up. Or said he had. Who would stand up a man like that? Maybe some *princesa* he was bringing in on his Lear jet from St. Moritz. Sidney hoped the *princesa* had eloped with the pilot.

But these fantasies were not getting one word of translation done. She pushed up her sleeves, sat down at her typewriter, and pulled the seedy copy of the California driver's manual towards her. She pulled her glasses down onto her nose from their perch on the top of her head and began pounding on the typewriter, putting the manual into Spanish. It wasn't very exciting, but it would keep her going for a while, maybe even get her VW out of hock. But she'd need something else to work on to get the roof fixed. Maybe Jock would come up with someone else.

Hours later, she was still at it, though nearing the end, when the doorbell rang.

"Damnation!" she muttered, getting up to look out the window to see who it was. She flung up the narrow little window and stuck her head out as far as she dared, but whoever it was, was standing too close to the door to be seen. Then she caught sight of a dark head and a leg in jeans. Brice! He'd forgotten his key again, she was certain.

"Drat you!" she yelled. "I'm right in the middle of something!" But she slammed the window down and trotted down the stairs anyway. She could use a break. She threw open the door, saying, "Forgot your key again, didn't..." Her voice trailed off. Philip Oliver was standing on her doorstep, in jeans and a blue-and-red rugby shirt. His green eyes held a glint of amusement as he looked down at her.

"You didn't give me one," he said.

"Oh, no, it's not my key. I mean it's Brice's key. No, I mean I thought you were Brice." Sidney stopped dead. She was babbling in surprise. Her hair was a mess, her feet were bare, and she was braless under the faded, ridiculous sweat shirt. She had her glasses on, her face was undoubtedly smudged with ink from the typewriter ribbon, and his sharp eyes were obviously noticing every one of these horrid details.

She took a deep breath, straightened up, and said, slowly, "Let me start over. I thought you were my neighbor. I keep a key for him because he frequently locks himself out. I apologize for yelling. What can I do for you?"

She was casting about in her mind, trying to figure out what he was doing on her doorstep. She decided that he must be lost. That was it. He wanted directions.

But instead, he grinned his devastating crooked grin and said, "I just happened to be in the neighborhood, and I just happened to have this bottle of wine, and I'd hoped you'd share it with me." He brought his hand out from behind his back and held out a brown paper bag. "But if I'm interrupting something..."

"No, no, not really," she said, astounded.

"My place or yours?"

"What?"

"Are we going to drink it here, or at my place? Mine's a little far."

Sidney finally realized that he was inviting himself into her house. "Oh, yes, come in," she managed to say, pulling the door open wider.

He stood in the center of her living room taking everything in. She tried to see it as he must be seeing it, the results of four long years of hard work—still unfinished—to restore the house inherited from her grandparents. The polished wood floors gleamed around the fringed edges of the worn Persian rugs. Heavily carved Victorian antiques, proud products of the jigsaw and lathe, mixed comfortably with more modern pieces picked up at secondhand sales. Her collection of South American Indian art—artifacts, carvings, statues—stood on the mantle and on the tables, and woven items were displayed on the walls. In a bookcase in the dining room, by the old piano, were her great-grand-father's books: fine old leather-bound sets of Dickens, Thackeray, Scott. On the stair landing stood her proudest possession, a tall grandfather clock that had come round the Horn on a sailing ship before the Panama Canal was cut. Like her house itself, the clock had survived the 1906 earth-quake. The late afternoon sun was coming through the stained-glass window she'd had made to replace the plain glass her great-grandfather had put in after that earthquake. It cast a diffuse multicolored pattern on the opposite wall.

"Nice, very nice," Philip Oliver said softly, as if she'd passed some kind of test. Sidney felt slightly annoyed, so she simply stood and said nothing. The room suddenly dark-ened, as the fog from the ever-present fog bank that stood out to sea began to stream past the windows. A distinct chill fell over them. Sidney walked over to a lamp and turned it on.

Oliver broke the silence. "You do like wine, don't you?"

"Yes."

He handed her the bottle in the brown bag. "It's just a naïve domestic Cabernet with no breeding, but I think you'll be amused by its presumption. I picked it up at the corner store."

Sidney couldn't resist laughing. She was glad he shared her sentiments about wine snobs, who seemed to have pro-liferated these days.

"I adore amusing little wines," she said, taking the bottle to the kitchen and hunting down the corkscrew.

By the time she'd opened it and returned to the living room with the bottle and glasses, he had laid and lit a fire in the fireplace. She'd managed to wash off her face in the kitchen and to achieve some order to her hair with a rubber band from her collection on the kitchen drawer-pulls. She put the bottle and glasses on the coffee table and sat down on the farthest corner of the couch. He poured the wine, handed her a glass, and sat leaning against the opposite corner. His eyes glittered in the firelight.

"Well?" he said.

"Well, what?" she asked.

"The wine. How do you like it?"

"Oh. The wine. Yes. A bit stemmy, but not as corky as one would expect."

"You read the same article I did."

"Yeah," she said.

The fog swirled. The sky darkened. The clock ticked. The cats dozed on the warm tiles in front of the firescreen. The level of liquid in the wine bottle went slowly and steadily downward.

"Okay," Sidney said. "I give up. Why are you here?"

"I told you. I was in the neighborhood."

"What possible business could you have in my neighborhood?" Sidney studied him out of the corner of her eye. He was sprawled languorously against the corner of the couch, looking into the fire. Until now, she'd not realized how well built he was. Thin, she thought, but definitely well put together. Graceful, but with a lean, wiry strength.

"Actually, I wanted to see how a deportee from Montgomery Street lived. A real San Franciscan." His white teeth were showing again, in a wicked grin.

"Oh? You're an anthropologist?"

"Strictly amateur." The clear green eyes ran over her face, her body, then back to her face. Sidney felt goosebumps rising. How ridiculous, she thought, and she shivered. She was suddenly conscious not merely of his good looks, but of something else emanating from him, a sexual magnetism deliberately directed at her. She feared that if she looked him directly in the eyes, she would freeze, hypnotized like a rabbit in the headlights of an oncoming car. Her mind, unbidden, leaped back to the time she'd met Max. He'd had that same quality, the frightening sexuality, the control over others, and especially over her. But, she quickly reminded herself, this man was not Max, and this man was way out of her class. She shook herself mentally.

"And what else are you doing here?" she said brightly, blousing out her sweat shirt so that it revealed nothing of her body. She wished she had run upstairs and put on a bra. "Are you offering me a job?"

"No. No job. I never mix business with pleasure. Cardinal rule number one."

"So this is pleasure?" Sidney said defensively.

"Isn't it?" he drawled. He paused and then added, "I owe you an apology for the other night. I should have made it clear that I wasn't going to hire you, before I took you to dinner. And I took you to dinner because I thought you were a most attractive and witty woman, and then I jumped all over you for being just that. That wasn't fair. Ernie's wasn't the right place to go, for me anyway. I'd like to do a replay—return to Go and start over. Will you come out to dinner with me tonight?"

Sidney was astonished. "You thought I was attractive in that ghastly suit?"

"Only because I guessed that underneath it was . . . a Forty-Niners sweat shirt." He laughed.

"Oh, damn," Sidney muttered, although she was pleased. Then she felt a hot flush rising in her body, and quickly turned away. The feelings she was getting were jangling her. There was some kind of electricity jumping between them.

"I don't know San Francisco very well. Surely you know some place we could go dressed like this?" Philip was saying.

"I'm not going anywhere dressed like this. But I can change, and yes, I do know some good places to eat."

"So change. It's getting late. I'll carry the wine and glasses to the kitchen."

"But we didn't finish it."

"It wasn't very good anyway. Just an excuse to come in."

They both rose at the same time and reached for the wine bottle. Their hands met on it, and Sidney said, "Oh, sorry," and made to let go of the bottle, but found instead that she was being pulled slowly toward him. She looked up in surprise, off balance, and saw those two green eyes burning into hers, and she was lost. He pulled her close against him, and her eyes closed; her chin came up and his mouth met hers. Her arms crept up around his neck, her body bent backward to press itself against his, in surrender or assertion, she did not know or care which. She felt him bend down a little to put the wine bottle back on the table, and as he did, his mouth moved to her neck, spreading fire, before he returned to her lips. Her mouth opened under the pressure of his, and then, as the strength went out of her knees, turning them to water, she felt his strong arms tremble, as if he could not hold her weight, slender as she was. She realized it was he and not she who was trying to keep control. Skyrockets went off behind her eyelids, her head reeled, and the earth moved . . . and moved again. He released her, and as he did, she heard a cacophony of clinks and rattles, and she saw that the bottle and glasses were toppling, walking across the tabletop. The pictures were swinging on the walls, the windows rattling ominously. The cats had disappeared.

"Earthquake!" he said. "Quick, get under the doorway."

When Sidney didn't move, he put one arm under her knees and picked her up, carrying her over to the arch between the living room and the dining room. She began to struggle urgently.

"Put me down!" she cried. The entire house lurched and came down with a bang, and things started falling in the kitchen and upstairs. She pushed against his chest, trying to get away, and he was forced to let go of her with one hand, in order to steady himself against the doorway. She broke away and dashed like a broken field runner across the room, toward the stairs.

"Come back, you little fool!" Philip shouted at her, starting to follow. But she had reached her goal before he could do more than take a few steps after her. The grandfather clock, its door hanging open, was leaning perilously, ready to pitch forward down the stairs. With a motion developed in long practice, Sidney slammed its glass door shut and threw a body block at the clock, pushing it back against the wall. Then she leaned against it, drained, as the house gave one more half-hearted lurch, sending everything rattling again.

Philip Oliver stood in the center of the living room, staring at her in amazement. "My great-grandfather never got around to anchoring it." Sidney explained. "We always had to do that." Then she remembered the scene in which the earthquake had caught them, and the weakness in her knees returned. She turned quickly and forced herself to go up the stairs.

"I'll just check for damage up here," she said hastily. "I'll be right down." At the top, out of sight, she leaned against the wall and devoted a minute or two to chastising herself. No one, not even Max, had affected her that way before. And now, this man, all but a total stranger, had with one touch caused her to throw all caution and good sense to the winds. Looking down at the clock on the landing, she thought: Great-Grandmother would say my behavior was indecorous, to say the least. As if in agreement, the earthquake's first aftershock jiggled the house and rolled on across the city.

CHAPTER THREE

DOLORES EDDY PICKED up the glass plates with the remains of the chocolate mousse on them, to take them to the kitchen "Finish the story, Sidney," she was saying. "I can hear you in the kitchen."

"Well, there isn't much more to it. After the earthquake, he left. He didn't want to have dinner after all. There was some damage, he said, at the labs in Sunnyvale, and he wanted to go down and see how bad it was. And I haven't heard from him since."

"More coffee?" Dolores was back, this time with a Georgian silver coffeepot, as elegant as she herself was. Sidney sighed inwardly. She'd always thought she ought to loathe Dolores. Dolores was beautiful, a tall, cool blonde, the kind of person that Sidney had always considered she, too, had inside her, trying to get out. Dolores, moreover, had dignity. She also had a successful career as a clinical psychologist, a handsome husband who was proud of her, and a daughter who was zipping through Stanford trailing straight A's and boyfriends. Dolores and her daughter looked like sisters. Dolores had decorated their condo like a professional decorator, threw parties worthy of Perle Mesta, cooked like a

French chef, did charity work, remembered everyone's birthday, read all the new books, took courses to keep up in her profession, skied and sailed. Despite all this, Sidney loved her.

Though Dolores was interested in Sidney's somewhat edited description of her misadventures with Philip Oliver, Jock, who had been present at some of it, was yawning. He stretched. "Sorry about the job, Sidney," he said. "I should have known it was a hopeless case. I'll keep an eye out for you for anything else that might come along."

He got up, taking his refilled coffee cup. "And now, if you'll excuse me, I'm going to watch the baseball game. I sense there is more to this story than meets the legal eye, Sidney, so I'll give you and Dolores a chance to talk about it, and then I'll take a deposition from Dolores later." He walked out, and a moment later Sidney and Dolores heard the TV go on in the den.

"He'll be asleep in ten minutes," Dolores said, laughing. "It's his turn to do the dishes, so I'll wake him up for that. Now, what's really going on?"

Sidney told her, in gory detail. She left out only the moment immediately prior to the earthquake, which she didn't want to think about much herself. She ended with: "He's such a gorgeous creature. A tasty morsel, as they say at Stanford."

"Well, be careful," Dolores said. "That's my advice."

"I already know that. But you're the shrink. What makes him tick?"

"I'd keep in mind the fact that he's recently divorced. You know what that does to people." Dolores had assumed, Sidney noticed, her psychologist demeanor. Warm, interested, but bland.

"That I know, too," Sidney said. "Good old Max."

"Does he remind you of Max?"

"No, not really. They're about the same age, but they're the exact opposite in looks. Max had the all-American innocent look. And blond. This one is dark and looks like a pirate. Also, don't forget I was eighteen when I met Max and nineteen when I married him. That's a big difference. I'm ten years older now."

"But you didn't find out what Max wanted until it was too late."

"I *still* don't know what Max wanted, unless it was a patsy. It certainly wasn't me, after the first few months. It wasn't more than a couple of years before he was chasing after the next undergraduate. Poor kid."

"Well, you must admit he was a dazzler."

"Sure, he was. He looked younger than he was, he stood up there in front of the class in his tennis sweater and his tan with his blond hair falling in his eyes, and he made even finance courses—present value of a future annuity, things like that—sound sexy. And afterward, there'd be his 'Let's meet at the park and go over your case study; it's too nice a day to sit here in this office.' I thought I was the only one who'd heard that one."

"And you graded his quizzes while he was holding office hours in the park, right?"

"Right. And did my own schoolwork, and ran the house."

"Sidney, while we're on the subject, how on earth did he ever afford his lifestyle on a professor's salary? I've always wondered."

"Consulting fees and inside information. He'd find some eager kid in his classes whose daddy was way up in a big corporation and find out there was going to be a stock split and zap!—in would go the margin order for a thousand shares. But he really liked consulting best. That way he could get his consulting fee *and* inside information."

"But isn't that illegal?"

"No, it was always legal. The SEC investigated one deal he was involved in, but dropped charges. But it wasn't ethical. He was never really dishonest, even with me. He *told* me about the undergraduates. It took me a long time to distinguish between those two terms—*illegal* and *unethical*. I think I'd prefer plain old dishonesty."

"Max still calls us occasionally, when he's in town. About every six months."

"Is he still teaching?"

"I don't think so. Just consulting. He always asks about you."

"And what do you say?"

"That you're fine, of course. I think he's more interested in how much your former condo, next door, is worth." Sidney and Max had lived next door to Jock and Dolores for the duration of their ill-fated marriage. In fact, Sidney thought, it was as neighbors that she, Dolores, and Jock had first met. "I think he wishes he'd hung on to it for more profit. Values have gone way up since then." Dolores looked sharply at Sidney, and her tone of voice changed. "Sidney, you should have taken your share in that divorce. Your pride has kept you from having a lot of things you could have had."

Sidney shook her head vehemently. "No. It was dirty money—unethical money. And it was his, and I wanted no part of it. He had no conscience. I had to live with mine. And I have, and I'm doing fine. But you know that. If it hadn't been for you and Jock living next door, I'd have gone bananas. I still miss you. I even miss crawling out onto the fire escape to borrow an egg.... But why are we talking about Max anyway?"

"Come to think of it, we were supposed to be talking about Philip Oliver."

"Yeah, I guess we were. Every time I think about him, though, Max keeps floating up. I don't know why. They really do seem to be complete opposites. I hope so, anyway."

"Think about that for a while, before you get involved with him."

"Dolores, that's just the trouble. I don't think I am going to get involved with him. He's a big shot, I'm nobody. He's rich, I'm not. I'm a klutz, he's a whiz kid. He probably has lady friends all over the place, so why would he be interested in me?"

"Look in a mirror sometime, Sidney. That might explain it. And there is one thing I know about him. He's a work-aholic. Jock told me. Mr. Chips is married to his company, and it's probably the reason his wife left him. That's a tough thing to live with."

"So you think it was all his fault—the divorce?"

"Probably not. I've heard she's an awful social climber. Always trying to get her name in the society columns, lunch at Trader Vic's, dinner at L'Etoile—you know the number. No wonder he doesn't like to go to Ernie's. She was trying to get in with the jet set. And I guess she's almost gotten there, too. Snagged herself a duke or a department-store heir. I forget which."

"Where'd you hear that?"

"I sometimes get beyond the comics in the papers, my friend. Try the society column sometime. Amazing what you find there."

Dolores got up, went to the kitchen, and pulled something from the cork bulletin board on the wall by the telephone. It was a newspaper clipping, which she handed to Sidney. "Like that, for instance."

Sidney was horrified to read the following:

SIGHT 'EMS: Who was the slick career lady seen with the elusive Mr. Chips at Ernie's Friday night? Rumors of Pacific Instruments being on the shorts since the great walkout last year leads knowledgeable Montgomery Streeters to think he might have a merger in mind. She's gorgeous, but is she rich enough?

"My God, Dolores, that's me!" she gasped. "That's terrible. What am I going to do?"

"Nothing. You can't do anything about it."

"But who told the newspaper?"

"That columnist probably slips one of the waiters a few dollars to tell him who's there with whom. Obviously, he didn't know who you were."

"Obviously. Slick career lady—in that suit! And the implication that he's after my money! That's almost funny. God, I hope he didn't see it."

"I imagine you'd have heard about it by now if he had. So you're probably home free."

"I feel sick."

"I shouldn't have showed it to you. I'm sorry, but I was afraid somebody else would first." Dolores looked a little rueful. "Let's talk about something else. Was there any earthquake damage at your house? What were you doing when it happened?"

"Oh," said Sidney, reddening. "Just drinking wine. I had to do my save-the-clock bit. There wasn't any damage. Some spices fell out of the rack in the kitchen and some bottles in the bathroom. I suppose this goes against your environmentalist sensibilities, but thank heavens for un- breakable plastics."

Dolores laughed. "As long as people aren't wearing them, I can stand them."

Sidney continued: "I noticed a big hole in your living room wall when I came in. Did the earthquake do that?"

"No, that's not earthquake damage. Just Jock's usual handyman efforts. He was trying to hang a mirror for me."

"But that hole is the size of a bowling ball! What was he trying to hang it with?"

"Who knows? Dynamite, maybe. I can't stand to watch him. Remember the time he decided to panel the den himself and drilled all those holes right through the wall into your dining room?"

Sidney began to laugh, and they continued swapping Jock stories until the subject himself came strolling back into the room, effectively putting a stop to their jokes with a hurt look.

CHAPTER FOUR

WHEN, THREE DAYS LATER, Philip Oliver still hadn't called, Sidney decided that it would be best for her mental health if she never saw him again. In an effort not to seem to herself to be hanging by the telephone in the exquisite anxiety of puberty, she plunged into a whirlwind of activities.

She finished the driver's manual and went down to collect the check herself, then went to rescue her car. While she waited in the shabby office of the garage, she found herself thinking about his dark hair and the way it just brushed his collar.

She translated a terminally dull treatise on gall bladders for a surgeon who intended to present it at an international conference, while recalling Philip Oliver's clear green eyes under the rakish brows, and how they crinkled when he laughed.

She provided interpreters from her contract pool for a Russian agronomist and a Thai general, and thought about his square jaw with the cleft in it, and the planes of his high cheekbones.

She went out with a former boyfriend, who took her to a crowded restaurant at Fisherman's Wharf and regaled her with stories about his job as a computer salesman, while she mused on Philip Oliver's wide, thin mouth and the whiteness of his teeth against his tan when he flashed his slightly crooked grin.

She asked Brice to help with the long calculations for her homework problems in her Operations Research course, and while wondering when she would ever need to know the most efficient way to stock a warehouse, tried to imagine what Philip Oliver's long, lean body looked like without any clothes.

She went to class one evening and was assigned four more problems designed to teach her the most cost-effective and timely way to build a nuclear submarine, and visions of his long-fingered, capable-looking hands rose in her mind.

From this, she determined that he was making her crazy. She began to hope that he wouldn't call. And, if he did, for her own sanity, she decided to say she wouldn't see him again.

Therefore, when he did call, apologizing charmingly for the delay, she accepted his dinner invitation immediately.

And spent hours getting ready. She'd neglected to ask where they were going, but decided it would be dressy. As he had seen her only in her prim banker's suit and her sloppy sweat shirt, she was determined to look as feminine as possible. She finally chose a low-necked, clinging blue-and-white silk print with long sleeves and a skirt that flared out at the hem. She tied a long white scarf around her neck, letting the long ends dangle dramatically. She was pleased with that effect, for it made her look taller, and she felt she needed every inch she could get. She felt dwarfed next to Philip Oliver.

She worked long and hard on her hair, and finally it fell in gentle curls, very fashionably, she thought, to her shoulders. Rather than risk smudges, she let the makeup go, except for a dash of pink lipstick. She slid small gold earrings into her ears, dabbed a drop or two of her precious Chanel Number 5 on her neck and wrists, fed the cats, and was waiting at the door, coat over her arm, when he rang the doorbell.

The effect must have been pretty good, she thought, for when she answered the door, his eyebrows rose and he looked her up and down for quite a while, finally saying, "Not bad for a Forty-Niner fan."

She took the opportunity to return the inspection. She deduced that the navy blazer must have been hand-tailored to fit the broad shoulders so well. The gray slacks, the blue shirt with a white collar, and the red tie were so trendy that she suspected him of reading *Gentlemen's Quarterly*.

"Not bad yourself—for an engineer," she said.

He laughed and put an arm around her shoulder to walk her to the car. It felt nice, she thought, and not at all dangerous. It was a good omen.

Once in the car, he headed in the direction of the financial district.

"I made reservations at the Carnelian Room. I trust that's okay with you?"

Sidney's first thought was that the waiters at the very fancy Carnelian Room were probably paid to tip off society columnists, too. Her heart sank.

"Well, I guess it's okay," she said dubiously. "We could go somewhere out here, though. I really wouldn't mind."

"You don't like the Carnelian Room?" he said, surprise in his voice.

"Oh, yes," she said hastily. "It's fine. It's great. Let's go there."

He shot her a curious glance and then concentrated on threading the car through the maze of weaving taxis and late commuters.

Another problem with the Carnelian Room was the fact that it was on top of the Bank of America Building, fifty-two floors up. Sidney was still clutching her stomach when the maître d' led them to a table in one of the window alcoves. It was an elegant place, all right, Sidney thought. She'd been in the bar, on the other side, a few times, but never in the dining room. The decor, unlike Ernie's, was elegantly understated, so as not to detract from the splendid view of San Francisco Bay and the Berkeley hills beyond.

Sidney looked very carefully at the maître d' when he seated them, removing the little RESERVED card that had been on the table. She decided he didn't look as if he talked to gossip columnists. Then she looked out the window and forgot about the elevator and the maître d'.

"Must be some view," Philip was saying. She had been gazing out, her nose almost pressed to the window. Embarrassed, she forced her eyes away. Below were the docks of the Embarcadero, beyond was Treasure Island, and on the horizon, Oakland and Berkeley, spilling up the hills of the coastal range. All were linked by the silver spans of the Bay Bridge. On the bay, a tugboat had cautiously nudged an enormous container ship along, among sailboats with furled sails motoring to their berths, and a gray navy destroyer knifed through the water under the bridge. A passenger liner was moored at one of the Embarcadero piers, sleek and white, with strings of flags flying from its funnel. Dusk was falling and lights were sparkling on at random everywhere.

"In fact," said Philip, studying her, "you look proprietary. Like you own it."

"In a way, I think I do," she answered, too seriously. Then she laughed to cover it up.

The waiter arrived with the menus and the wine list. Sidney fished in her purse and found her glasses, in order to read the menu, but seeing that her copy had no prices on it, she decided to let him order for her. She was afraid she'd pick out the most expensive thing on the menu. Then she thought how silly that was. Someone as rich as Philip Oliver was supposed to be wouldn't even notice.

He ordered artichokes vinaigrette and veal cordon bleu, both favorites of hers, and a recent Robert Mondavi Pinot Chardonnay. He did not pretend to be a wine connoisseur, for he relied on the waiter's suggestions. That she liked. It was delightful that he was not pretentious.

Over the artichokes, the conversation turned to politics, and though they belonged to different parties, they agreed on most issues.

Over the cordon bleu, they got to sports. Sidney had to

confess that her 49er shirt was a sham and that she really didn't follow any team very much, and Philip said that the extent of his interest was to get into the company baseball pool during the World Series. She further confessed that she was generally inert, in terms of exercise or individual sports, but would really love to learn how to sail, and he explained that his daily set of tennis was mainly to keep in shape, not for any great love of the game.

She was surprised to learn that he read a lot. "I never met an engineer who *could* read," she teased. She quickly asked what newspapers he read, and was relieved to learn that the *San Francisco Chronicle,* with its society column, was not among them. Both hated "how-to" and self-help books. Both loved Tom Wolfe and Kurt Vonnegut. He liked Updike, she Didion. He liked symphony but not opera. She liked the symphony and didn't know if she liked opera, as she couldn't afford to go. They agreed that *Evita* was the best musical they ever saw. He liked Woody Allen; she didn't. "Too New York," she said. They both liked Crosby, Stills, Nash, and Young, Tom Lehrer songs, and anything by Noel Coward.

Night had fallen by the time they reached dessert, and the view from the window became magical. The black bay was ringed with city lights, like a necklace of diamonds. Sidney discovered that she could see Philip's reflection in the window, so, pretending to watch the lights of the cars moving across the Bay Bridge, she studied him, only half-listening to what he was saying. She could see him in profile and decided she liked that particular view best. The high-bridged nose, the strong chin, the nearly black hair, the set of his shoulders, the way he moved: everything was right. She liked the cut of his clothes and the easy relaxed way he wore them, clearly unconscious of how handsome he was. To top it off, she was thinking, they had found an amazing range of agreement on a variety of subjects. But she suddenly realized that he had stopped talking, so she looked directly at him, to find he had that wonderful grin on his face.

"What's so funny?" she asked innocently.

"I was doing that earlier," he said.

"Doing what?"

"Watching your reflection in the window. Very rewarding."

Sidney flushed. "Oh, but I wasn't—" she started, but he cut her off by signaling the waiter.

"Two Courvoisiers, please," he said, and then, as the waiter hurried off, he crossed his arms on his chest and gazed at her with a little smile. The look in his eyes was so lustful that Sidney wanted to squirm. Feeling her face getting hot, she cast around for something to say, and said the first thing that came to her mind.

"Uh, I forgot to ask: was there any serious damage from the earthquake?"

Immediately upon saying it, Sidney could have bitten her tongue, for he said, with heavy innuendo, "Nothing permanent. I'm sure we can carry on."

He leaned across the table, but the waiter arrived with two warmed snifters of cognac, forestalling him. He leaned back with a wry look.

"Have you bolted your clock down yet?"

That seemed safer ground, so Sidney said, "No. I keep meaning to do it, but it's one of those things you just keep putting off."

"Isn't a hundred years long enough to get around to it?"

"I guess I am a little lax."

He was smiling broadly again. "You know, you Californians *are* from another planet. You know perfectly well that there's going to be another big earthquake, and you don't take the slightest precaution. You even brag about living on the fault line. No wonder Woody Allen thinks you're flaky."

"Well, what else can we do about it?" Sidney said, a little stung. "Come to think of it, Sunnyvale must be right on the San Andreas fault. What have you done about it?"

"For one thing, we've made it earthquakeproof—it was designed that way. But here in San Francisco, everything's built on sand. And look out there." He pointed to the Embarcadero. "Everything from Montgomery Street to the bay is built on landfill. One big quake and it'll all go."

"We made it through 1906, we'll make it through the next one."

"Eat, drink, and be merry, you mean? Because tomorrow the City falls on your heads? That's been the motto here ever since the Gold Rush. Isn't that the laid-back San Francisco way of doing things?" His voice was teasing, but there was a hint of seriousness behind it.

Sidney flared. "Right. We're all laid back and smug and snobbish about our culture, which as you New Yorkers know, we haven't got anyway. And we aren't all hustling somebody else twenty-four hours a day to make money, and we haven't got the Metropolitan Museum of Art, so you think we're second-rate. Or have we gotten that far up the scale? Are we even third-rate yet?"

"I didn't say that, you did." He was grinning at her anger.

"Admit it, you would have if I'd given you the chance. I've heard it all before. You people move out here and then yearn for the Big Apple, and tell us how inferior we are. But you stay on." Sidney was glaring at him now.

"I'll admit I think San Francisco is overrated. Or it overrates itself. I think it's trying to compare itself to New York, which, if you'll pardon the expression, is comparing apples and oranges."

"How often do you come to the City?"

"As little as possible."

"Have you ever been to the neighborhoods, where the real people live?"

"No."

"Then you don't know anything about it."

A long silence fell over the table. Sidney stared out the window. This time she was really looking at the cars on the bridge. She chastised herself for bringing the subject up, and then remembered that she hadn't—he had. She knew she was narrow-minded about her city . . . just as New Yorkers were about theirs. She decided to apologize.

"I'm sorry," they said in unison. He grinned engagingly

and said, "Pretty silly thing to argue about, isn't it?"

"I agree."

"It's still early," he said. "Let's go someplace else. Where to now?"

Sidney thought for a minute. "How about Peter Mintun?"

"Who, or what, is Peter Mintun?"

"He plays the piano. He knows everything Noel Coward ever wrote."

"In that case, let's go," he said.

The only sensible thing to do to get to the bar where Peter Mintun played was to take the cable car. They rode on the exposed outside seat, with Sidney taking quick glances at Philip under her lashes to see what he thought of this inefficient and ramshackle but very San Franciscan means of public transport. He seemed to be enjoying it.

"I'll bet this is the first time you've ever ridden one of these, isn't it?" she said.

"No bets. You're right."

L'Etoile, at the top of Nob Hill, where Peter Mintun played, was jammed, as usual. But they were lucky. Another couple was leaving just as they arrived, and for once nobody was waiting to get in. The place was dim and small and furnished with small, low tables and vaguely Victorian settees and chairs. But nobody ever thought about the decor, for everyone came to hear the slender, blond young man seated at the big black grand piano, which took up a good portion of the room. While Philip ordered drinks, more brandies, Sidney looked around the room. She saw a few familiar faces, none that she could put a name to, and not a single tourist. Peter Mintun was a San Francisco treasure, and those who knew about him kept it to themselves. Even so, the bar at L'Etoile was always full.

He was wearing, as always, a dinner jacket, black tie, and black patent shoes. His hair was parted in the middle and plastered down, and he wore small gold-rimmed glasses, evoking the slightly decadent elegance of the twenties and thirties.

Like everyone else, Philip was delighted. "He's wonderful," he said. "Where did he learn all those songs? He's too young to know them."

"His parents had a collection of records from the twenties and thirties. He grew up with them. He got a music degree from some university, and he's said to be a good classical pianist, but he prefers this."

And, on Philip's request, Peter Mintun played Noel Coward. He started with "Mad Dogs and Englishmen," went to "Sail Away" and "Mad About the Boy," segued into "Don't Put Your Daughter on the Stage, Mrs. Worthington," and then played "I'll Follow My Secret Heart."

The songs and the brandy and the atmosphere washed over Sidney, making her nostalgic for an age she'd never known. When Peter Mintun played a couple of songs she didn't know, she saw that Philip did, for he smiled in recognition at each one.

Peter Mintun ended the evening with "Let's Do It." They left, reluctantly, Sidney humming. While they waited for the cable car, they had a small argument about whether Cole Porter or Noel Coward had actually written "Let's Do It," and concluded that Porter had written it and Coward had added to it. Then they sang as much as they could remember of "Mad Dogs and Englishmen" just because it was the most absurd thing one could sing on top of Nob Hill on a chilly, clear night.

The grand hotels around them were floodlit and had flags flying, the doormen still busy, even though it was past midnight. There were honking taxis, occasional limousines, cable cars rattling past. There had apprently been a high school prom in one of the hotels, for the sidewalks were full of boys awkwardly resplendent in rented tuxes and girls glowing and happy in their party dresses. In the midst of all this, Philip leaned down and said, "I guess there *is* something special about San Francisco after all," and right then and there, as the cable car creaked to a stop, he grabbed her and kissed her until she thought she could never breathe again. Then he swung her up on the cable-car step as easily as if she were a feather and jumped on behind her. The gripman smiled knowingly. Even though the car wasn't crowded, they opted to stand, hanging on the outside, laughing.

It seemed only appropriate, Sidney thought, to invite him in for a nightcap when he brought her home. In fact, he seemed to expect it. While he looked through her record collection, she went to the kitchen to fix drinks.

"Scotch okay?" she called, and he said, "Fine. Make mine on the rocks." She splashed Scotch over ice cubes in two glasses and put a generous amount of water in one of them. She'd already had, she decided, somewhat more than her limit on drinks tonight.

She handed him his drink, and she saw that he'd taken off his blazer and loosened his tie. The music was on very low, and there was only one light turned on in the living room. It seemed only natural to sit side by side on the couch, shoulder to shoulder, thigh to thigh, sipping the Scotch and feeling the warmth of his body.

Then he put his drink down on the coffee table and said, "Give me your drink."

Without thinking, she handed it to him and he put it beside his on the table and in the same motion gathered her into his arms.

Looking deep into her eyes, he said, "Let's do it!"

"Give me a good reason to," Sidney said, knowing what would come next.

"Well, how about: Barnacles and clams do it."

"Not good enough."

"Other species without hands do it." He kissed the tip of her nose.

"More," Sidney said.

"More what?"

"Reasons."

"Japanese tourists with their Nikon cameras do it." He kissed both of her eyes.

"And who else?"

"Gypsy moths and Medflies when feeling amorous do it . . ."

She was laughing now, and he tried to stop it with his

mouth. And succeeded for a moment, until she wriggled out from under.

"What else?"

"Computers with their little chips don't yet do it."

"Greek heiresses who own lots of ships, they won't let do it."

His hand was now brushing against her breasts, and the kisses became more searching. She did not try to escape, nor could she have, for every nerve in her body was crying out with the need of him. But still she said, when he lifted his head, "You're going to have to convince me."

"I know. I'm thinking," he said huskily. "Whales swimming past Point Reyes do it . . . Waiters with champagne on trays do it."

With that verse, Sidney felt the zipper on the back of her dress being pulled down, and she was, at the same time, unbuttoning the buttons on his shirt. She moved, helping him pull the dress from her shoulders, aching to feel his smooth skin against hers. His breathing was growing ragged as she ran her hands over his neck and back, but he continued:

"Supreme court justices in their robes do it . . . In fairy tales princesses and toads do it."

With the smoothest velvet touch, he had her bra off and was cupping a breast. "Beautiful," he said, and kissed the hollow of her throat, and then, as she arched back, his mouth found her nipple, teasing it with his tongue. Flames shot through her.

His hands moving expertly, he looked up.

"More?" he said, green embers burning in his eyes.

"Yes, oh, yes," Sidney gasped.

"Okay," he said, grinning. "Toll takers on the Golden Gate do it . . . In L.A. the second-rate do it."

"No, not more of that." Sidney pulled his head down to her mouth. As he kissed her deeply, her breasts were in delicious contact with his chest.

He stopped and unwound her arms from around his neck. He stood up, then reached down and scooped her up in his arms.

"Time to go upstairs," he said. Sidney looked up at him and something in her brain went click, and she saw the face of a complete stranger. A sudden sick feeling in the pit of her stomach overtook her, and she went limp in his arms. Her skin felt clammy and cold.

"What's the matter?" Philip said in concern.

"I don't know. I think you'd better put me down." The room was taking on a new aspect, a strangeness, as if she had never seen it before. She was overwhelmed with a feeling of being totally lost, of being in the wrong place at the wrong time.

He put her down gently, and she leaned against him, shaking, for a moment, and then she began pulling her dress up.

"Are you ill?" she heard Philip say.

"I don't think so. Something happened. I feel . . . weak." The lost, homeless feeling was leaving her, and he no longer looked like a stranger.

"I'm sorry," she said, and meant it. "I guess I'm just not ready for that. I have to sort some things out in my head. I wouldn't blame you if you were angry."

"I'm not angry," he said. He was putting on his shirt. "You're probably right."

"I don't just go leaping into bed with people, you know," she said, the words sounding inane even to her own ears.

"I'm sure you don't," he said, smiling, his composure obviously restored.

He knotted his tie, put on his coat. It was now all Sidney could do to prevent herself from running to him and saying, "Please don't go." But pride had become involved, and she could not. His reasonableness had put her on the defensive.

"You sure you'll be all right?" he said, looking at her carefully.

"I'll be fine."

He kissed her on the top of her head. "I'll call," he said over his shoulder as he went to the door.

Sidney watched from the window. Her heart in her throat, she waited till his car had pulled out of sight. She couldn't rid herself of a dreadful sense of loss. Finally, she turned off the lights and went upstairs. She undressed and slid, naked, between the chilly white sheets of her bed.

She stared at the ceiling for a long time. For a moment there, she'd thought she'd lost it. That she was going crazy. At that precise moment when Philip had lifted her . . . "Time to go upstairs," he had said. But lying, hands crossed behind her head, she remembered other times she had felt that same physical reaction. That awful strangeness. She had felt it as a child when she was doing something she knew was wrong. Not necessarily wrong in itself, perhaps, but wrong for her. It was, she supposed, her conscience. She groaned and buried her head in the pillow, just as Cole Porter's refrain popped into her head. "Let's do it," her mind sang. "Let's fall in love."

CHAPTER FIVE

THE ENTRANCE TO San Francisco Bay, the world's largest natural harbor, was called The Golden Gate. At its very tip was Land's End, the northwesternmost piece of land in San Francisco and the southern hinge of the Gate. It was a hostile place, because the winds there were so fearful, the cliffs so sheer, and the waves so violent. But it was a place of breathtaking beauty, too. Or so Sidney McKenna thought each time she saw it.

Just south of Land's End, at Point Lobos, Cliff House, the third or fourth version of it, clung to the headland, just as it had since the Gold Rush days. But others who built there had sooner or later come to grief. The ruins of the mansion Adolph Sutro built stood on the highest point, surrounded by cypress trees bent to the contour of the hillside by the constant fury of the wind. Below, on the ocean's edge, stood what were once the Sutro Baths, a vast complex of covered saltwater swimming pools, now also in ruins. From Point Lobos, Sidney could see across the entrance of the bay to Point Bonita, with its pure white classic lighthouse, and the Marin headlands rising high and stark behind it. Farther north, lost in the mists, was Point Reyes, graveyard of galleons, and beyond that, a dangerous, bleak, rocky coast that stretched, nearly deserted, a thousand miles to the next deep-water harbor.

In front of Cliff House, out in the open sea, stood Seal Rocks, a group of minute, craggy islets where sea lions occasionally appeared, but which most often were a roosting place for thousands of cormorants. In a storm, the waves crashed over the rocks and drove the birds and sea lions away. One of these rocks was connected by a narrow crumbling stone causeway to land. If one were brave enough to go past the faded brown sign that said: …CAUTION. CLIFF AND SURF AREA EXTREMELY DANGEROUS. PEOPLE HAVE BEEN SWEPT FROM THESE ROCKS AND DROWNED; if one were to walk very carefully, putting one foot exactly ahead of the other and never looking down at the raging surf on both sides, one would reach this rock. Mostly, only determined fishermen did this. Now Sidney, leading a wary Philip Oliver, had done it.

On the rock, the footing was very bad, as always, for, as always, it was wet and there were no flat places either. Sidney and Philip picked their way carefully. It was just sundown. They seated themselves.

They were alone, the last of the fishermen having gone home. The tourists, who had peered out at the rocks and the ocean from the stone battlement above and behind them on the cliffs, had long since clambered into their buses or gone to ground in the Cliff House for food and drink. The last of a flotilla of oil tankers and freighters that had streamed out under the Golden Gate Bridge on the outgoing tide was disappearing into the gray fog bank out to sea. The first fingers of fog were curling into the entrance to the bay. "Very nice," said Philip. "You can believe I would never have done this on my own."

Sidney smiled slightly. Then, giving in to an overwhelming urge, she demonstrated one of her linguistic talents: she barked. And so, in return, did the sea lions, sitting out on the white rocks.

"Now do James Cagney," Philip said.

"Sorry, but I only do seals." Sidney leaned back against the hard slippery rock behind her, bracing her feet on an outcropping. Her hair whipped back from her face, and she could taste the salt spray on her lips. She wore jeans, a heavy sweater, and a tweed jacket, but even this was not enough. It was still cold. She pulled her jacket collar up in a futile attempt to get warm.

"Cold?" Philip asked, sliding over as best he could on the cramped sloping ledge on which they had perched. He put one arm around her shoulder, very carefully, for fear of knocking them both into the vicious surf below.

"Well, you know what Mark Twain said." She grinned.

"Yeah, I know. The coldest winter I ever spent was summer in San Francisco, that's what he said." His tanned face was very close to hers. "We *can* go, you know. Nobody's making us stay out here."

"Just a few more minutes," Sidney begged. "This is my kind of place."

"It's a crazy place. I nearly killed myself getting out here. You didn't tell me to wear climbing boots." He looked wryly at his loafers.

"You didn't tell me you were coming into town today, either."

"I didn't decide until the last minute."

"What made you?"

"I haven't taken a day off in a while."

"But what made you decide to come to the City—to call me?" Sidney persisted.

"You fishing?"

"I guess I am."

"Okay. First, I find you refreshing and funny. Second, you're good to look at. Third, I think we'd be fantastic in bed together."

"Oh," said Sidney. "Well, at least you're straightforward." She moved over as far as she could.

"I've been left with the impression," Philip continued, "that you might agree."

Sidney rose. A gust of wind caught her and pushed her

back against the rock. She bent over and held on to it, and began walking carefully back toward the causeway.

"It's time to leave," she said. She had the advantage. She had worn hiking boots, which clung to the rock. She was on land before he had even started over the dizzying causeway.

Directly ahead of her rose the cliff up to the road. The Sutro Baths had been built into its banks, and there were concrete blocks and twisted steel beams scattered at various levels. She'd climbed here many times and knew that the main difficulty was loose sand. With boots, she'd have no problem. She started up, kicking steps like a mountain climber in a snowfield. Halfway up, she looked back and saw that Philip had chosen to take the longer, easier trail. She was at the top, dusting the sand from her hands, before he even reached the base of the cliff.

What did you expect, she said to herself, a protestation of love and a marriage proposal? Did you think he would say, "I came into the City because I am madly in love with you, you're the most beautiful woman I've ever seen in my life, and I want you and only you for the rest of my life"? Come off it, Sidney. At most you're an interesting diversion, like an occasional game of squash. And what about you? You've never played the reluctant virgin before. You know how the game is played.

And you asked for it, she resumed lecturing herself. You practically jumped into bed with him the first night, and you probably would have, had it not been for the earthquake. Why should you suddenly feel crushed because this one man says what all the others only hint around about? Wasn't it just the other night that you were talking about honesty? Now you've got an honest man on your hands, and you can't handle it.

She watched him as he walked up the gentle slope. He'd appeared suddenly, early in the morning, out of the blue. "Show me the real San Francisco," he'd said, and she had. They'd started out in Golden Gate Park, in the morning fog, wandering past the pristine white glass Conservatory, which stood among its formal gardens like a child's dream of Victorian England, and gone on to the Academy of Sciences, where she'd had a terrible time tearing him away from the aquarium and the planetarium and the Foucalt pendulum. She'd insisted on walking around Stow Lake, and he'd insisted on renting a rowboat and rowing around it. They'd done both. They'd gone on to the De Young Museum, where she'd been amazed that he knew art and pleased that he'd liked their quiet lunch at the small café. The sun had come out, and they were able to have their sandwiches and wine outside at the glass-topped tables under the umbrellas around the fountain.

They'd driven down to Fort Point, built during the Civil War, its spiked guns guarding the Golden Gate, now dwarfed by the titanic red span of the bridge. They'd watched the waves slide around the bridge's south tower and smash against the sea wall. From there, they'd driven slowly up the long sweep of the coastal cliffs, through the eucalyptus and cypress trees of the Presidio, pausing for the heart-stopping views of the bridge and the headlands. At the Legion of Honor they had stopped to see the collection of French Impressionists housed there. The rest of the afternoon had been spent climbing around the glorious ruins of the Sutro Baths.

It had been a lovely day. The conversation had been easy and amiable, about nothing in particular. Every place Sidney had taken him was as familiar to her as the palm of her hand, and she'd been surprised, at first, that almost all of it was new to him. He had meant what he said: he didn't come to the City unless he had to. He'd seen the financial district, Fisherman's Wharf, and a few fancy restaurants. She'd asked him, "But what have you been doing all these years down in Sunnyvale?" and he'd said, "Working, just working." Subject dropped.

Two things she'd especially enjoyed: his surprised exclamations at the sheer beauty of her city, for she knew that he was seeing it through her eyes; and the admiring glances of the people they passed, for she could read in their eyes that she and Philip were a handsome couple, he with his dark head bent over her, she with her eyes sparkling.

Now he was walking up the path toward her, his shoulders hunched against the wind. His hands were in the pockets of his windbreaker, and he was looking at the ground, watching his footing. He looked, she thought, vulnerable. At last, a few feet away from her, he looked up and met her eyes. Her heart turned over in her chest, and she knew that the problem was that she was falling in love with him. And that made her the vulnerable one, not him.

He took her arm and said, "You looked like a mountain goat going up those cliffs. Do you do that all the time?"

"Only when I'm upset, thank you," she said, pulling away.

"Come on. I promised you dinner." He took her arm again. "We'll talk about it." He cocked his head down at her, and with a grin that had lost its piratical effect and was now merely boyish, said, "Please?"

So she went helplessly along. The fog was overtaking the entire western end of the City, and as they drove through the shrouded streets Sidney could hear the foghorns. She explained that that was one reason why she loved living in the avenues—you could hear the foghorns. The avenues, she explained, were the middle-class neighborhoods that ran from the midpoint of the City to the ocean to the west, bisected by the long green strip of Golden Gate Park.

The restaurant Sidney had chosen was on Clement Street, the main shopping street serving the area. Clement was lined with hundreds of small shops, restaurants, and service places, most of them reflecting the ethnic mix of the City. There were Chinese greengrocers, Russian bookstores, Arab spice stores, French bakeries, Italian shoe-repair shops, and restaurants ranging from small but elegant Continental to shabby Korean. Clement was not, Sidney explained, tourist territory.

Philip was circling the block for the third time, in search of a parking place.

"This is the *real* City," she said.

"I'm beginning to realize that," he said, as he waited

patiently for the driver of an ancient Pontiac to realize that the parking place he'd appropriated was too small for his car. "I can fit into that one, if he'd just give up."

Sidney could never remember the name of the restaurant, and with good reason. The owner changed it every few months, in hopes of attracting a larger clientele. But it never worked, and the same loyal group, of which Sidney was a part, always ate there. Sidney and Brice referred to it as the "Armenian Place." It stood on a corner, across from a store that specialized in wicker furniture and always had a "Going out of Business" sale on, and beside a printing shop with dusty, twenty-year-old wedding invitations in the window.

The decor was early attic: mismatched tables and chairs, wallpaper appropriate to a Victorian insane asylum, and startling, garish pictures of dancers in Armenian costume, posed stagily before painted snowcapped peaks. What the restaurant lost in ambience, it made up for in portions of food, which consisted mainly of such items as ground lamb on a skewer, ground lamb on a sourdough bun, ground lamb in pita bread, all sprinkled with sumak, a bland red spice. Sidney loved the place and considered it hers. So did a small number of other regulars.

The owner's wife, who doubled as hostess and waitress, greeted them at the door and seated them at one of the tables by the front window. Because Sidney was a steady customer, two glasses of red wine appeared on the table, gratis, while she explained the intricacies of the menu. They settled on something entitled azna kebob, Sidney's favorite—a kind of Armenian hamburger, served with salad, heaps of saffron rice, and slices of cheese and fresh fruit.

It was impossible to carry on a conversation of any length in the Armenian Place. Aside from the food, that was the reason she had chosen it. As she'd expected, the proprietor, taking time off from his duties as cashier and supervisor of the steaming kitchen, came over and sat with them for a few minutes. He asked if they liked the new name of the restaurant. Sidney thought it ghastly, but didn't say so. It had not, she learned, brought in any new customers.

Philip, who had complimented Mr. Saroyan on his establishment and his food, waited patiently until the elderly Armenian had returned to his post, and then said, "Now, let's have a little talk."

But at that moment two couples sat down at the next table, and Sidney recognized one of the men as her plumber. He remembered Sidney well, for he had spent several days tracking down a gas leak in her attic. The leak, he explained in detail to Philip, had been due to the fact that the entire house was once lit by gaslight. The outlets for the gas had been plastered over aeons before. It was the pipes leading to these missing gas fixtures that were leaking. Philip, Sidney could tell, was fascinated.

"Sidney, I really think..." he was saying, just as one of her down-the-street neighbors spotted her. The neighbor came breathlessly over to the table, saying, "I've been trying to get you all day. There's a public hearing tomorrow night, at the Park and Rec Department, about diverting traffic down our street on Sundays. We're trying to get as many people as we can from the neighborhood to go speak against it. Can you go?" Sidney said she could, and the neighbor returned to her own table.

Sidney explained to Philip that the woman was the president of her neighborhood association. He nodded.

"I can see that we aren't going to—" he began, as a pair of blue-uniformed policemen parked their squad car outside and came clanking into the café. Sidney recognized them as being from the Sixth Avenue Station, in her area, and excused herself to go talk to them about the traffic diversion. They were against it, too, and agreed to go to the Park and Rec hearing. The policemen ordered coffee, and Sidney returned to her seat, explaining to Philip that he was seeing grassroots democracy at work.

Evidently feeling temporarily defeated, Philip devoted his attention to getting the check and easing Sidney out. Just as they stepped through the glass door, a big, red-faced, friendly-looking man pulled the door back and held it for them. "Hi there, Sidney," he said. Philip took her arm, obviously intent on preventing any more discussions of gas leaks or traffic diversions, but the man continued into the restaurant and began shaking hands with the owner.

"I suppose that was your dentist?" Philip said.

"No, actually, it was my state senator."

Philip started laughing. "Did you take me there on purpose? So we couldn't talk?"

"No," Sidney lied. "I took you there so you could see what real San Franciscans are like. Now you can say you've been in the neighborhoods."

"I certainly can," he said with some irony in his voice.

At her door, Sidney quickly unlocked it and stepped through, whirling to close it partway before he could enter. She looked up at him with her most innocent smile.

"Thanks for a lovely day. I really enjoyed it. And now, if you'll excuse me, I have a busy day tomorrow." She started to close the door.

But he was too quick for her. "Oh, no, you don't," he said, jamming his loafer into the door. "You and I are going to have a talk."

"I can't imagine what we have to talk about," Sidney said disingenuously.

"If you don't let me in," he said with a devilish grin, "I promise you that not only will *you* know what we have to talk about, but so will your neighborhood association."

"You wouldn't," Sidney protested, but she could tell from the look of him that he would. "Well, in that case, you may as well come in."

She opened the door a bit wider, and he stepped in.

"Want me to build a fire?" A quirk of his dark eyebrows made it more than a simple question.

"No, thanks," Sidney said briskly, making a circuit of the living room, turning on every light. "I don't think you'll be staying long enough to make it worthwhile."

He walked over and switched on her stereo. It was set on FM radio, and the Muzaky strains of "Moon River" poured out, flooding the room in saccharin. Sidney quickly switched it to a hard-rock station.

"I can offer you coffee or water," she announced.

"How about some of that cognac over there in the cabinet?" He nodded toward the dining room. "I'd have saved that before the clock in the earthquake."

"Okay, okay." Sidney grabbed the cognac, a gift from a grateful lawyer who believed that her ability to interpret his client's stuttering Spanish had saved his case, on her way to the kitchen. She found, by rummaging in the back of one of the cabinets, one brandy snifter, and into it she sloshed some cognac. When she returned with the single glass, Philip had turned off most of the lights, and the radio was playing something romantically classical, which Sidney couldn't quite place at the moment. He himself was sitting on the couch, in the exact position he'd sat in before. He'd hung his windbreaker on the coat rack in the foyer, and his long, lean frame was sprawled comfortably, his feet on the coffee table. Sidney handed him the cognac and seated herself on the very edge of the chair opposite him.

He sipped the cognac and then, swirling it in the glass, looked first at it, then at her. He started at the top of her head, and finished with her feet, and when he got through, she felt stark naked.

"Nice. Very nice," he said.

"I've always heard that Remy Martin was the best," Sidney agreed, deliberately misunderstanding. She couldn't afford to let the need for him that radiated through her every nerve become noticeable. He was, she knew, deliberately doing the masterful male number. She'd seen it often, if in slightly different form, in Max. It was the stuff of Love 'em and Leave 'em, a game she could not play, not with this man. The next thing he is going to say is *Come over and sit by me,* she thought.

"Come over and sit by me," he said, in the tone he might have used to an employee who was on disciplinary probation.

"No, thanks," she replied.

"Don't you trust me? Or is it yourself you don't trust?" He took another swig of cognac and looked right through her. Her heart took a leap and ricocheted off her rib cage.

"Yes. To both," she said. "I don't trust either one of us."

"So I gathered. Isn't that rather silly, considering that both of us are adults? This isn't high school anymore."

"No, it isn't. I went to a convent school, all girls, in Caracas. It wasn't like this at all."

"I can tell by the way you're sitting on that chair. You might as well have on your uniform and knee socks. Very ladylike."

"And what's wrong with that?"

"This is California. You aren't supposed to be a lady. You're supposed to be in touch with your feelings, find your own space, relate to other people, get wired into the lifestyle. Have I got it right?"

Despite herself, Sidney had to laugh.

"That sounded pretty good."

"I have a good ear for dialect," he said.

"Look," Sidney said, "since you are so anxious to go to bed with somebody, why don't you advertise in one of those papers out there? You have the vocabulary for it. You know, 'Professional man wishes to meet person to share his space and help work through his feelings. Unattached female preferred, but will consider anything.'" She tried to soften the words with a smile, but it didn't quite work.

He finished the Remy Martin. "I'm trying to be a little more selective than that." He stood and walked around the coffee table, pulling her to her feet as he reached her. He held her at arm's length, his hands on her shoulders, looking down at her, searching her face. She stopped breathing and ordered her senses to control themselves. The effort to do this made her close her eyes, so she didn't see him bend down, but only felt his mouth on hers, probing, testing, exploring. She could taste the cognac on his lips. The music was building to a full and triumphant climax. He pulled her close, and she could feel the muscles working in his chest and the strength of his arms around her. She fought for control as he kissed her cheek, her throat, her mouth. She could not resist, but she would not, she swore to herself, respond.

Suddenly, he released her and held her again at arm's length. He looked her up and down again, and then he grinned his wicked, lopsided, buccaneering grin, loaded with sex.

"Once more, with feeling," he murmured, and this time the lips that covered hers were more than exploratory. There was no tenderness, no attempt at subtlety. The kiss was one of raw power, of sheer domination. She felt among her jumbled emotions—no, not emotions, mere flashes of impression. But before she had time to define them clearly, the kiss had ended and she was merely cradled in his arms, gently, protectively, her head against his chest, so close she could hear the slow, steady beat of his heart.

His deep, clear voice rumbled in her ear: "I'm not very good at psychology or, as Californians say, getting into other people's heads, but I know there's something scaring you. That reaction you had the other night—that was a fear reaction if I ever saw one."

Sidney pulled back and looked into his face, trying to read it. There had been some fleeting expression there, but she could not tell what it was.

"Yes, it was fear, I suppose," she admitted.

"But fear of what? Me?"

"The last time I felt that way was the day of my wedding. It's fear of commitment," she blurted. As soon as the words were out of her mouth, Sidney knew them to be true.

"But I'm not asking for commitment," he said, reasonably.

"I know," she said wryly.

"So that doesn't make any sense."

"I know."

He gently set her back down on the chair, got his windbreaker, and put it on. Sidney did not see any of this, for she was sitting rigidly with her back to him, but she could feel every movement he made, as if it were projected on her nerve endings. He returned, looming behind her, and put a hand gently on her shoulder.

"I'll be in touch," he said. And then he left.

Sidney didn't stand to see him to the door. She sat for a long time, looking at the empty snifter and letting the music wash over her. She realized now that she was hearing the last movement of Beethoven's Ninth Symphony, the *Ode to Joy*. She switched it off in the midst of a triumphant chorus, picked up the snifter, and went to the kitchen. There she rinsed out the glass, poured herself a shot of the Remy Martin, and carried it upstairs to bed with her. The cats followed, frolicking up the stairs at her heels.

She assumed she would never see Philip Oliver again.

CHAPTER SIX

THREE WEEKS LATER, Sidney found herself once again on the bus, going downtown. Her car was working, but she couldn't afford to park in the Financial District.

After a long silence, Philip Oliver had called and left a message on her answering machine. When she'd returned the call to a Pacific Instruments' number, he'd asked her to meet him at Tadich's on Thursday at eleven-thirty. It was business, he'd said. Strictly business.

It was terrifically hot, Sidney thought, at least seventy-five degrees by 11:00 A.M., meaning that it might get to eighty that day. People would be collapsing on the street. Anything over seventy degrees Fahrenheit was a severe shock to a San Franciscan's system. She put on one of her few hot-weather outfits: moss-green cotton blazer, green-and-white seersucker skirt, white frilly blouse. She could not commit the cardinal San Francisco sin in dressing, which was wearing white shoes, for she owned none. Forsaking the Nikes, she'd put on brown pumps. And this time she'd remembered her glasses and her certificates.

The City sparkled under the bright sun, refreshingly at first, and then, as the heat grew more oppressive, the pastel

Mediterranean colors assumed a flat, ugly glitter. The faintest trace of what nobody would ever have admitted was smog had turned the cloudless sky into a hard, coppery blue. It depressed Sidney. She tried to open the bus window, but it was stuck shut. She gloomily wondered why, when it rained, the bus windows were always stuck open. Then she wondered, for the hundredth time, just what it was Philip Oliver wanted. Was he, against all reason, going to offer her a job? And why had he chosen Tadich's, which even he must know was the sine qua non of the ambitious three-piece-suiters of Montgomery Street?

Tadich's had gotten its start selling drinks to gold miners and hadn't really changed much since. It had a long, polished bar, brass fittings, and big, elegant mirrors. Its walls were paneled in mahogany. And even as early as eleven-thirty, when Sidney punctually arrived, it was jammed. But she found Philip easily, in one of the back booths. She'd half-expected to find someone else with him, a referral, perhaps, but he was alone. She'd also half-expected to see him in the ominous pinstripe suit, but today he wore pale gray. He had, she noticed, almost the only tan in the place. She deliberately plastered a big smile on her face and slid into the seat across from him.

"Hi! How's everything in Sunnyvale?" she said flippantly.

He didn't even smile. Nor did his handsome face show any emotion at all, merely impassivity. He said brusquely, "Fine. Let's order now and get it out of the way."

The next few minutes were taken up with ordering, and the delivery of water and baskets of bread and butter plates. Finally, when lunch had arrived and the waiter had been assured that they didn't need anything for a while, Philip spoke.

"For a number of reasons, I hate to do this. I'll explain in a minute. I have some documents here in Spanish and Chinese that need translation. Would you look them over and give me an estimate of how much you'd charge to do them? Yourself, I mean, not one of your subcontractors."

Sidney looked up in astonishment. "Me? You want *me* to translate them?" She stopped eating, her fork halfway to her mouth with a marinated calamari on it.

"To be honest, I didn't want you to do it. But I looked all over for a substitute for you, a replacement, and I learned Jock Eddy was right. You're the best in town, for this particular job." He nodded at the calamari on her fork. "I'd suggest you either put that thing in your mouth or back on the plate." There was just the faintest trace of humor in his voice.

To her regret, she opted to put it in her mouth, and it was chewier than the rest, so that her next question lacked the incisive diction that dignity and her injured pride required.

"If I'm the best mmmm in town, mmmmh why didn't you hire me in the first place? mmmmh Damn," was how it came out.

"Possibly because you talk with food in your mouth." His face was deadpan, but there was a faint gleam in the green eyes.

A flash of anger, mixed with some other, indefinable emotion, gave Sidney great difficulty in swallowing, but the recalcitrant piece of squid eventually got itself past her epiglottis and allowed her to speak. Her face, she knew, was flushed.

"I have to know your reasons for not wanting to hire me before I can make any decision on your sudden, flattering offer, Mr. Oliver. It's only fair, if we are going to have a contractual relationship. I do require a signed contract, you realize?" Her voice was as flat as it was possible to make it.

"I realize," he said. "I'm perfectly willing to explain my reasons to you, and I'm sure you'll understand them. There were two: first, I was afraid that you couldn't keep your mouth shut. You'll have to admit that I got the distinct impression, when I met you, that you were less than discreet with information. The second reason is that I don't believe in personal involvements in business—and I mean that on a man-woman basis. Aside from what it can do to your judgment, there are far too many awkward legal problems that can come up. Such as sexual harassment."

Sidney's head had come up at the words *sexual harassment*.

"Wait a minute—" she started to say, but he forestalled her.

"There are plenty of crude ways to put it. 'Fishing off the company pier' is one of them. Any contract I sign, any employee I hire, or for that matter, anyone who hires me, should be under what they call an 'arm's length transaction.' I made that mistake once and I'll never do it again."

"And those interesting reasons no longer exist, in this case?" Sidney said, as nastily as she could.

"I think not," he said flatly.

"So all transactions should be arm's length? But a few weeks ago—that wasn't what you were talking about or acting on then." The minute it was out, Sidney wished she hadn't said it. It sounded defensive, smacked of hurt pride.

He said levelly, "I think, much as you or I might like it otherwise, that once we are under contract, the most intelligent thing to do would be to keep it at arm's length. I'm sure you'd agree." His eyebrows rose, and a calculating look came into his eyes. "You wouldn't want it any other way, would you?"

"Of course not. You're absolutely right." Sidney attempted several more bites of the spicy calamari, which she loved ordinarily, but they seemed flat and tasteless. She was confused. Not about what he was saying, but about her own reactions. Here he was offering her a terrific job, as well as removing himself as a problem to her, and the treasonous thought was crossing her mind that she'd rather have him, even if for only a short time, than any job.

Sidney swallowed and said, "Okay, then, why am I the sole beneficiary of this offer?"

"Also for several reasons. As I said, I checked around. You do have the reputation of being the best. But other than that, you have a unique combination of languages, Spanish and Chinese. In a deal like this one, the fewer people involved, the better. It must be kept on a 'need to know' basis. I'd have to hire two or three people to handle what you could do alone. That's one or two more people involved who needn't be. I'm sure you see the logic of that."

"Of course." Sidney chewed that over for a minute, along with a buttered piece of sourdough bread. "I have one more question, though."

"Shoot," he said.

"What was your big mistake? You fished off the company pier?"

Anger crossed his face for a moment, making his mouth a thin line, but it was quickly followed by the same bland expression he'd maintained throughout the discussion.

"That's something you don't exactly have a need to know," he said slowly. "But yes, I suppose you could say so. I married my administrative assistant. It was a disaster, for a number of reasons."

Sidney barely restrained herself from saying, "But you must have loved her." She thought she'd seen a fleeting expression of pain in the anger, so she said instead, "Sorry, that was way out of line. I shouldn't have asked that."

"Not your fault. I shouldn't have brought it up. My error," he replied politely and with an air of finality. "Now, would you like to take a look at these?"

It was his turn to rummage in an attaché case, and he brought out a thick folder of papers. "This is just the beginning. There will be a great deal more later, and I'll probably need some interpreting, as opposed to translating. There will be negotiations. Give me a time frame on these, if you can."

Sidney took a big swallow of ice water from the heavy stemmed glass in front of her and reached for the folder. She put on her glasses. She took her time, looking over the papers carefully, and saw that they were some kind of offers or specifications in regard to setting up assembly plants. The words *taxes, ministry, labor,* and *multinational* leaped out at her. She had been right that night at Ernie's.

"This *is* a lot of work. Surely these were also submitted to you in English?" she asked.

"They were. But they were done by people who were not native English speakers, in their own countries. We want them retranslated, to make sure that every word means what it is supposed to mean. Those are just starting positions. The contracts will come later."

"How much time do I have?" She was calculating mentally.

"Well, I'm no different from anyone else. Yesterday will do. As quickly as you can, at any rate." He said it with a faint smile.

"I'll have to farm out everything else." Sidney was thinking out loud. She found her calculator and plugged in some figures. When the numbers came up in the window of the calculator, she decided she had the decimal point in the wrong place, so she did it again. But it was the same figure. It would take care of her living expenses for a long time, supply a new roof for her house, and leave plenty for a trip to Peru to visit her parents. And maybe even contact lenses. She was afraid to say the figure aloud, so she turned the calculator around so that Philip Oliver could see it and said, "I can do it in one month, and it'll cost you that much."

He barely glanced at it. "Fine. Here's the contract—fill it in." He handed her a long, legal-looking sheet. She saw that her name was already typed in.

"I'll have to get Jock to look it over first," she said.

"He's the one who drew it up. I asked him to."

"You discussed all this with him before you discussed it with me?" Much as she liked Jock, Sidney felt her privacy had been invaded.

"Not really. I was in his office, talking about something else, and asked him to draw up a contract that would protect your interests as well as mine. I thought it might be a selling point."

"You really want me to do this, don't you?" she asked, looking at him very hard over the tops of her reading glasses.

"Frankly, yes."

"Okay, You've got yourself a deal."

He seemed relieved, she thought.

But she read the contract first. There was some dissension

on a detail or two, and some more paper shuffling and some discussion of logistics. She was to keep in touch, making progress reports by telephone directly to him, and she was to have the translations delivered by messenger when complete. Sidney's head was bent over as she signed the contract, so she saw nothing, but she sensed that Philip had moved slightly.

"Well, hi, stranger," came a familiar voice.

Sidney's head snapped up, and she saw a tall figure in a three-piece suit, carrying the inevitable leather attaché case.

"Brice!" she said, startled.

"You didn't tell me you were going to be down here today," Brice said accusingly. "In fact, I haven't seen you all week."

Philip Oliver, she noticed, was looking at Brice warily.

"Mr. Oliver," she said quickly, "I'd like you to meet my neighbor and good friend, Brice Lorraine. He's a commercial loan officer at California National Bank. Brice, this is Philip Oliver, Pacific Instruments."

Brice looked faintly startled but recovered himself and stuck out his hand, so the expression was covered by the rigmarole of polite greetings.

"Sorry, I didn't mean to disturb you," Brice apologized. "I'm meeting a client for lunch, and it's so unusual to see Sidney here. . . ." His voice trailed off.

"That's okay," said Philip Oliver. "We were through transacting our business. As a matter of fact, I'm just leaving. Nice meeting you, Mr. Lorraine. I trust I'll be hearing from you soon?" This last was directed at Sidney.

She nodded, and then glared at Brice while Philip picked up the papers strewn on the table, snapped his attaché case shut, and left.

"Why are you mad at me?" Brice said pleadingly.

"You knew darn well who that was, you hypocrite!" she snapped.

"No, I didn't. How could I have known that was Mr. Chips? I've never laid eyes on the man before. And what was that all about, anyway?" Brice went on the offensive.

"Something very big. I'll tell you about it tonight, when you get home. You owe me a drink." Sidney didn't see the curious looks cast by several bystanders, in response to this exchange, because she, too, was snapping her attaché case shut and shouldering her way through the crowd.

CHAPTER SEVEN

THE NEXT MORNING, Sidney plunged right in. She spent a couple of hours clearing the decks: passing on other commitments to her subcontractors, canceling those that she could cancel. She had rearranged her little office, putting away everything that was not relevant to what she was doing, and was now sitting at her desk with the photocopies of the Chinese documents before her. She'd started with the Chinese because it was the hardest, had the most words that did not translate easily, and had the greatest number of nuances. She tapped a pencil on her teeth and ran her eyes down the columns of ideographs, getting the gist of the thing, letting the language flow through her head, only half-thinking about it.

As she'd told Dolores over the phone the evening before, Sidney didn't understand why she was so displeased with what had happened. Dolores, had been right: Philip Oliver was dangerous—to Sidney anyway, considering her feelings about him, which she had finally been able to define. She hadn't met anyone like him since Max, and that had been catastrophic. She could very easily fall head over heels in love with Philip, but he had made it clear that he was not about to get involved in any long-term commitments. Or short ones, either. And a casual affair was out of the question. It would be anything but casual on her part, and she couldn't afford that.

Now the problem had solved itself: she didn't have to worry about it. He wouldn't get involved with an employee, and considering his experience with his ex-wife, he had good reason not to. And now she had this fantastic job, which he'd given her, albeit grudgingly, on her own merits. She'd finally have enough money to do some of the things she desperately needed to do, and it would be so nice to have a cushion. She'd forgotten how nice. And, she confided to Dolores, she could see that the job might lead somewhere, in the direction her whole life seemed to be aimed. Even Max had been part of it, if involuntarily. She wanted to do consulting work—international consulting. And here she was, with her first offer. Well, almost-offer. Translation was a foot in the door. And other Silicon Valley companies would be going multinational. The field was wide open.

So why was she so unhappy? she'd asked Dolores. Dolores said only, "I think you've answered your own question," and Sidney said, "Right. I've got this silly schoolgirl crush. I'll get right to work on it. Hard work and time will cause it to go away." And Dolores said, "Of course," but there was a funny note in her voice.

Brice, naturally, had been pleased for her. He deduced far more about how she felt about Philip Oliver than she'd told him, and disapproved. "He's way out of your class," he warned her on several occasions. "He's a jet-setter." He refused to believe her protestations to the contrary. "Prove it!" he demanded. Sidney had to admit that she knew next to nothing about Philip, didn't know where he lived, didn't know what he did in his spare time, didn't know who his friends were. "You're just jealous," she said. But she knew that Brice was right, for Philip Oliver had deflected almost every personal question she'd ever asked him. He was a very closemouthed individual. (But what a mouth, she thought, what a smile.)

Upon hearing of her new job, however, Brice had gone into some flights of fancy, featuring Sidney in boardrooms all over the world, giving incisive advice in nine languages to captains of industry and presidents of medium-sized countries. "I wish I could type," Brice had said. "Why?" she'd asked. "So I could go with you, as your secretary. I've always wanted to fly around on corporate jets."

The ringing of the telephone brought Sidney back to reality. She'd drifted completely away from the translation and into her own recollections. And, she now realized, she'd forgotten to flip on the answering machine, so as not to be disturbed. Cursing a bit, she picked up the phone and listened to a spiel about buying a magazine subscription. "No, thank you," she said and, hanging up, switched on the machine. One of the cats was sitting contentedly on top of her typewriter when she returned. She chucked him out the door, a little unkindly, she realized, and then relented and let him back in. "Stay on your side of the room, Gregory," she told him. "I've got work to do." She sat down again and began in earnest.

It was immediately obvious what these papers were. Pacific Instruments, as she'd guessed, was attempting to open a plant overseas. Though she could not tell from these documents the exact nature of the product the company intended to assemble in the projected plant, she could tell a great deal about its plans. Background documents in English had been included. Someone—a New York firm, to be exact—had already done some scouting, in fact a lot of it. The consultant had settled on three countries as the best possibilities.

Sidney sat back, reflecting. There were hundreds of things to take into consideration, she knew, besides cost. Things like the skill and educational level of the labor force, the stability of the government, the availability of transportation, the nature of the competition, and any restrictions on foreign investors. Third World countries were growing rapidly wiser in the ways of protecting their own interests.

The papers to be translated were the second step in the "scouting" process: they were offical descriptions from government ministries of what each country would require of Pacific Instruments, and what the country in turn could offer in the way of tax breaks, infrastructure, finance, site locations, and so forth. The next step would be the actual negotiations, Sidney knew. There were consulting companies that specialized in these things, including negotiations. She devoutly hoped she would get to sit in on some of them.

Within a week she had done almost half of the Chinese document and shipped it off to Sunnyvale. Determined to finish as quickly as possible, she'd worked through the weekend (who ever said that self-employment was easier than the corporate life? she said to Brice in one of her rare moments off) and straight through the next week. Her shoulders ached from bending over the typewriter, but her first check had arrived, and the size of it had widened her eyes and caused her to redouble her efforts.

She cut her Operations Research class. What was an M.B.A. compared with the real stuff? Brice barged in and lectured her about eyestrain and general sloppiness in other areas of her life. She relented a little and took him out to dinner at the Pacific Café for rex sole, feeling very flush. Brice made a lot more money than she did, but he had huge mortgage payments, and she did not. She felt very charitable.

By the end of the third week, she knew how it would come out. It was obvious that one government was making by far the best offer, even though she knew only one side of it. As she whipped through the translations, she remembered that she wasn't supposed to come to conclusions about things. Her job was merely to translate, not give advice. At least not yet. If she wanted to be in on the negotiations, she'd have to be very careful about that, she reminded herself. And she'd have to be careful about another aspect of it: not discussing with anyone what she was doing. Brice could give her lots of basic information, but she hadn't asked him, though she was terribly tempted. She was also terribly tempted to question Jock on the stock issue, but she knew better than to do that. She was becoming expert in resisting temptation, she thought wryly.

At the end of a month she was done. She called Sunnyvale and was almost relieved to hear that Mr. Oliver was out of town. He had left word that he would contact her as soon as he returned. She called the messenger service and dispatched the last pages of her translation, along with the originals, and slumped in a chair, wondering what to do next.

She'd take a few days off, that's what she'd do. Soak in the bathtub, take a long hike on the headlands in Marin, maybe invite the Eddys for dinner. But first she'd spend some of that money.

She was dialing the roofer when the doorbell rang, and when she went to answer it, Philip Oliver himself was standing there.

Without preface he said, "I've got some more work for you." He was wearing a dark suit. His tan had faded, and he looked tired.

"Oh?" Sidney said, not knowing what to do next. Did he want to be invited in? Was that kosher? Her heart had done just a little flip-flop, a very minor one. Just surprise, probably.

"I could use a cup of coffee, if you've got one," he said, evidently noting her uncertainty.

"Sure. Come on in," she said, and he did. "I just sent off the last of the Spanish translations," she told him over her shoulder, heading for the kitchen.

He followed her and sat down wearily at the kitchen table. "Good," he said.

He looked, she thought, very out of place sitting in her kitchen. As she put the tea kettle on and measured the coffee into the pot, he said, "I was on my way home from the airport and thought it would be easier just to drop this stuff off."

"Where have you been?" she asked.

"New York."

"Business or pleasure?"

"Business. Seeing the consultants."

"And how did you find New York?"

"Hyper. God, I don't know where they get the energy.

Everybody's hustling. All they care about is money and how to make more of it."

Sidney could not resist taking a dig at that. "So the former New Yorker thinks things are better here in laid-back Lotus Land?"

"I'm not quite ready to admit that," he said with a smile, "but I've begun to see certain advantages. I thought about that rock of yours out there in the ocean a few times. While I was sitting in traffic jams breathing exhaust fumes and sweltering. The taxi's meter was ticking, and so was the consultant's."

Sidney poured boiling water into the percolator. "Would you like a sandwich or something?"

"No, thanks. They fed me on the plane."

"You look tired."

"I am. I got up at four this morning. The reverse red-eye special."

"But I thought you'd have a company plane!"

"We thought about it, and it wasn't worth it. Cheaper to fly commercial."

Sidney poured the coffee, carried the two mugs to the table, and sat down opposite him. "Okay, what have you got for me?" she asked.

"More of the same," he answered. "These are directed toward tax rates, fees, exchange rates—financial stuff. It should be easier—more figures."

While Sidney pored over the photocopies, he called Sunnyvale. She wasn't really listening to what he said, but she heard him give something that sounded like orders to a secretary and then heard him say, "...be in later." The work did look easier. Depending on when he wanted it, she could probably still take some time off.

When she looked up, he was back in his chair, sipping coffee and looking somewhat revived. He was, in fact, looking more than revived. He was looking at her speculatively, she thought.

"I hope you don't expect me to start on this today," she said. "I just finished the last batch, and I worked straight through weekends. I'm taking a day or two off, I hope."

"No problem. You have a couple of weeks before the conference."

"The conference?" she echoed.

"We're starting discussions, I hope, in two weeks. The minister of industry of Piedras Negras, the man we want to talk to, just happens to be coming to the U.S. on a vacation. I'm looking for a place where we can talk without interruption, with no distractions. The minister speaks English, but I want you to be there. You may be able to pick up something we can't. I presume you'll be available?"

Available? Sidney's mind was whirling. Of course! Here was the dream starting to come true—like Brice's crazy fanstasies. Though a minister of industry of Piedras Negras wasn't exactly the president of a medium-sized country, he'd do.

"Yes, I think I can schedule it in," she said coolly.

"You understand, though, not a word to your friend Bruce or whatever his name is. Or anybody else. This is top secret."

"My friend's name is Brice. And I don't talk to him about it. Or anyone else. I'm so discreet that I've even forgotten what I translated." She smiled.

"Good," he said. "You'll do." Suddenly the big, buccaneering grin was back on his face. He stood up and walked to the door. She went with him, and as she opened the door, he turned and looked down at her.

"Sidney, I . . ." He stopped. His expression had changed subtly, and he seemed to be leaning toward her.

"Yes?" she said, her heart pounding in her chest. "Yes?" she repeated.

But he caught himself, with a visible effort. "Thanks for the coffee," he said, and he went down the steps to his car, without once looking back.

It wasn't until later that Sidney realized Philip's "dropping by" had taken him thirty miles out of his way.

CHAPTER EIGHT

CALIFORNIA 1, THE Pacific Coast Highway, is narrow and twisted, and Sidney nearly shot past the Timber Cove turnoff, which loomed up suddenly on a sharp curve. The difficult part of driving this way, she was thinking, was that it was so beautiful you had a terrible time keeping your eyes on the road. Sometimes it ran along the continent's edge over sheer drops, and at other times it streaked inland over fog-nurtured rangeland or wound through the pine-clad, low mountains of the coastal range. It had taken her well over three hours to drive this in the VW bug. She'd been up the north coast many times but had never stopped at Timber Cove Inn. In fact, she had never seen it.

Philip Oliver's secretary had called a week before, saying that the meeting would be held at Timber Cove Inn, as a convention had booked up all the San Francisco hotels. Sidney was to be at Timber Cove by Thursday afternoon. Reservations had been made for her in the name of Pacific Instruments. Sidney should plan to stay approximately five days.

She'd said she would be there. Had the secretary been less impersonal, she would have added, "With bells on."

As it turned out, Timber Cove Inn stood only a few yards back from the road, a long, low building nestled among rocks and trees, made of glass and hand-hewn redwood beams, weathered and graying. Sidney's was the only car in the small, graveled parking area, and when she walked into the lodge, she found herself entirely alone.

This main part of the building was two stories high, and above her were parallel balconies, in elaborately carved wood, running the length of the room. Behind these balustrades were doors that Sidney guessed opened on bedrooms. Directly in front of her as she entered was an enormous stone fireplace two stories high, covering most of an entire wall. To her left was a glass wall through which she could see a small artificial pond, with cattails and water lilies and giant orange carp. To her right was a long bar and the reception desk and the dining room. As she looked around, searching for a clerk—or any sign of humanity—Sidney glanced at the dining room and the wall of glass beyond it. Outside the floor-to-ceiling windows was a green meadow, and beyond that a rocky point of land, dropping sheer into the crashing waves of the gray Pacific. Atop the rocky point was a statue, or rather an enormous pillar of smooth concrete, painted at the rounded top with the face of an Indian woman. It was, Sidney knew instantly, a Bufano. Benny Bufano had been San Francisco's most beloved sculptor, noted for his wise and witty and often monumental works.

Tearing herself away from the view, she began wandering a bit in the dim, cavernous room, calling "Hello" a little timidly down corridors. No one answered. Eventually, she saw a pot of coffee on a warmer and some mugs, and saw, too, that there was a blazing fire in the fireplace, and heard the soft classical music that was being piped in. Seeing nothing better to do, she poured herself a mug of coffee and sat in a deep, comfortable leather couch, from which she could see both the fire and the tossing ocean. Slipping off her shoes, she put her feet on the generous coffee table, took a few sips of the delicious, fresh coffee, and promptly fell asleep.

"Are you charging this time to the company?" A deep, clear voice woke her.

Sidney's eyes flew open, and she found herself looking directly into the green eyes of her employer, Philip Oliver. Though she could never have explained why, she knew that he had been watching her for a long time as she slept. She had a sense that her privacy had been invaded, and she saw a knowledge of herself in his eyes that quickly swept away all traces of sleep.

She felt her cheeks redden, and she jumped to her feet, knocking her coffee cup over and the coffee into her shoes. As she bent to pick up the brown loafer, she heard the voice again:

"So the curse is still in effect?"

"Looks like it," she said ruefully, wondering what to do with a shoeful of coffee.

"I hope you have your Nikes with you."

"Oh, lay off will, will you?" she said with real feeling. She was thinking seriously of throwing shoe and coffee at him.

But he was too quick for her. He went to the bar to find a towel and helped her clean her shoes.

"Thank you," she said.

"My pleasure," he replied. "Why aren't you checked into your room?"

"I couldn't find a living soul around here," she answered, but even as she said it, she saw that the desk was now manned, a bartender was behind the bar serving three or four people, and waiters were busy in the dining room, setting tables.

"Really?" he said, looking around the room quizzically. "Well, in any case you can check in now." As he turned to leave, he added, "Dinner's at eight."

A little apologetically, she checked into her room. The man at the desk told her she'd looked so comfortable that no one had had the heart to wake her, which embarrassed her. But when she got to her room, which was at the farthest northern end of the inn, in a wing attached only by a covered outside walkway, she forgot her embarrassment.

The room had one entire wall of glass overlooking the
ocean. Before it was a small table and two chairs. A bed
covered with a homemade quilt stood against the rough
redwood wall opposite. The floors were wide planks, covered with hooked rugs, and there was a glass-enclosed shower
that also overlooked the ocean. From the smaller front window, Sidney could see the mountains, with stands of pine
rolling off into a high blue horizon. But the room was
dominated by a fireplace, in front of which lay a luxurious,
thick, earth-toned hooked rug. Stacked beside it was what
must have been a week's supply of oak logs. There was no
TV, no telephone, no radio. Simply the bed, the view, and
the fireplace.

Sidney unpacked, and took a long shower—so long, in
fact, that the windows were steamed over. She put on gray
wool slacks, a pink, white, and gray striped sweater, and
tied her hair back with a pink scarf. Then she went outside
to explore the green meadow. She walked to the cliff ov-
erhanging the ocean and watched the waves crashing on the
rocks below. She stopped to pick some wild poppies. The
sun was just beginning to set on the horizon, and Sidney
wished she were here on vacation rather than at work. It
was, she thought, a place for relaxation, a place for thoughtful solitude. No, not that, she realized. It was a place
for . . . lovers. She felt suddenly bereft. Clutching her small
handful of flowers, she headed back inside.

A few people were already in the dining room—three
or four couples at scattered tables. But the only person at
the bar was Philip Oliver, and he and the bartender seemed
to be deep in conversation. She stopped for a moment and
looked at him. He had lost his earlier pallor and was as tan
as ever. He wore a white turtleneck Aran Isles sweater,
brown slacks, and topsiders. He looked gorgeous, and perfectly at home. As she watched, the bartender said something to him and he laughed, throwing back his dark head.
Her heart turned over.

Watch it, Sidney, she said to herself. She advanced to

the bar, bouquet in hand. She slid onto the stool next to Oliver.

"Where is everyone else?" she asked.

He turned to look at her. It was a long, calculating look, and while he looked at her, the bartender drifted away. She could not meet his eyes and, not knowing what else to do, looked first at the red sunset, then at her little clutch of golden flowers. Her pulse was racing. It was ridiculous. She felt like a schoolgirl.

At last, he said, "There are no others. We're the only ones here."

That brought her head up. She looked into the depths of his green eyes, trying to read them, but there was nothing there by this time. Just blandness.

"Why not?" she ventured.

"The minister's plane was late, so they decided not to drive up until tomorrow."

"Oh," she said.

"What do you want to drink?" he asked.

She settled on what he was having. That turned out to be a gin martini on the rocks, Tanqueray, of course. She remembered that once she'd been able to swing a bottle of Tanqueray, when she'd been feeling especially flush. Brice had drunk most of it, over a period of several months. She discovered that she liked it, now that she wasn't paying for it.

They sat quietly, sipping their drinks and listening to the Chopin études coming from discreetly hidden speakers. There was a quiet murmur of talk from the diners, and several others had appeared at the bar, claiming the bartender's attention.

Finally, Philip said, "Dinner?"

"I guess so."

They went into the dining room and were seated at a small table for two, near the window. The menu was French, though the waiters were all Vietnamese. Sidney put her little bouquet of poppies down by her silverware and studied the listings. She decided on a mushroom salad and petrale sole stuffed with tiny bay shrimp. Closing the menu, she looked out the window at the setting sun. It was quite spectacular.

Philip, too, stared out the window. His mood seemed uncharacteristically pensive.

For the first time, Sidney became aware of the low hum of conversation around them, of the clatter of dishes in the kitchen.

Philip turned sharply, meeting her gaze. "Did you have any trouble finding the place?"

"Not really," she said.

The waiter approached, moving silently, unobtrusively. He waited expectantly, pad in hand.

They gave their order. Philip requested a carafe of the house white. Sidney nodded her agreement. The waiter wrote it all down.

Calm and gray, the sea stretched out before them. The lower rim of the sun was just touching the horizon, and a golden streak of light seemed to Sidney to be leading directly toward her, across the surface of the water. "Nice sunset," she said.

"Yes, it is," he replied.

In what seemed like no time, the waiter set their plates down before them.

"Looks good" was Philip's comment.

Sidney agreed.

The waiter poured the wine.

They ate in silence for a while. As the sun dropped below the horizon, it appeared to increase in size, until it was an enormous golden semicircle. The sky had turned a pale pink, fading into yellow.

"There will be seven others coming in tomorrow," Philip said.

"Really?" Sidney replied without much interest, though she knew that she ought to be picking up on every bit of information she could.

The waiter came shyly up with a pressed glass vase for Sidney's flowers.

"Thank you," she said, and slipped the flowers into the

vase. Philip poured more wine.

"Don't you want to know who's coming?" he asked.

"Yes, of course," she said, as brightly as she could, but her voice lacked conviction. Philip looked at her sharply.

"First, the minister of industry of Piedras Negras," he said. "He's bringing three aides and a secretary. Then the New York consultant and his administrative assistant."

"Good," Sidney said. "That sounds very interesting."

They declined dessert. The sun had dropped below the horizon and disappeared fast. For just a moment the sky glowed like molten gold, and then it was dark.

Coffee finished, Philip said, "Big day tomorrow. Time to go to bed."

She searched for any extra meaning there, and found none. After he had signed the bill, she stood and said, "Thanks for the dinner. What time do you want me in the morning?"

His eyes roved over her face for a moment, but he said only, "I'll let you know. And don't thank me; it's a business expense. It comes off my taxes."

"Of course," she said. And she went to her room. Her loafers clacked hollowly on the wooden floor of the balcony, and when she opened her door, the room looked dark, lonely, and bleak. As she stumbled around the room looking for the light switch, she realized that she'd foolishly brought nothing to read. Having slept that afternoon, she was now wide awake. She finally found a small lamp beside the bed. It cast a small, warm glow over one corner of the room. She noticed that the fireplace was laid, so she searched out a packet of matches and lit the fire. It blazed up, strong and warm, and then she noticed that the drapes had been drawn over the windows.

She pulled them back and stood watching the moonlit ocean below. A wind had come up, and the trees outside were tossing. She could hear them rustling above the faint boom of the surf. She felt totally alone. Was this, she wondered morosely, what it was all about? Her first taste of the big time, the top of the heap, the international corporate world? This was where she'd always wanted to be, privy to great secrets, near powerful people. Then why was she so sad?

There was a knock, very discreet, on the door. The maid, thought Sidney, but when she opened it, Philip stood outside. He held her little vase of flowers in one hand and a brandy bottle in the other.

"You forgot your flowers," he said, handing them to her.

"Thank you," she said.

"My place or yours?" he asked.

She groaned. "Not that again." But her pulse was racing.

He smiled down at her, his eyes hooded. "It's too early to go to sleep. I'm sick of going over position papers, and I need company. May I come in?" The smile broadened into a grin, and her heart turned over. "You're the boss," she said, opening the door wider, though warning bells were ringing in her mind.

"That's the right idea," he told her. She took the flowers to the table beside the bed, while he looked for glasses in the bathroom. He found two and poured an inch of brandy into each.

"By the window okay?" he asked, and she heard something like shyness in his voice. Her head was spinning. Was this to be another arm's-length transaction?

They sat at the little table, and while he sipped his brandy, she watched him. The firelight brought out the sculpted planes of his face, the slight hook of the nose, the shadowed, deep-set eyes, and the very size of him, she mused. He seemed lost in thought.

Sidney took a big swallow of brandy, which burned her mouth and brought tears to her eyes, but then turned silky and smooth and slid coolly down her throat, bringing a warm glow that spread out through her veins to her fingertips. It's like the fire, she thought, taking another sip.

"Sidney." Now he was looking at her. His face was solemn, his eyes unreadable. "I don't understand you," he said.

"I don't understand myself," she replied.

Then she thought she heard him say, "To hell with it," under his breath.

"What?"

But he said, "Hold still. There's something on your face." He put his hand out touching her eyebrow. Automatically she closed her eyes tight as he rubbed at her temple with his index finger.

And then suddenly she felt his lips on hers, felt him stand and pull her to him. He cradled her head in one hand, holding her against him with the other, his mouth never leaving hers. At first she was so startled that she could neither resist nor respond as his eager mouth gently explored hers, the darting tonue playing in and out while his hand moved along her back.

Pulling away, she gasped, "I thought you said—"

"Whatever it was, I didn't mean it," he said, pulling her close again and kissing her eyes, each in turn. "I need you."

Those were not the words she wanted to hear, and she struggled to pull away from his embrace and that long, taut body that was beginning to attract hers like a magnet.

"No, no," he murmured into her hair. "Go with it. It's right.

"I can't," she wanted to say, but by then she was lost. Every sense was on fire, magnified, exquisite. The firelight gave a different cast to his face, making it gentler, taking the hard, piratical edges away. She could taste the tang of the brandy on his mouth, smell the faint clean smell of him, and feel, oh, the things she could feel. She felt the roughness of his sweater on her face, the warmth of his smooth skin under her hands, the springy, thick hair on the back of his head, the strength and the leanness of him against her softer body, against her swelling breasts. And she could hear, too. She could hear the slow, hissing thunder of the surf on the cliffs, the rattle of the wind against the windows, and the crackle of the fire, and most of all she could hear his heart, beating more and more rapidly.

Holding her away from him, pinning her arms at her sides with his hands, carefully keeping space between them, he bent his head and kissed her slowly, gently, sweetly, a kiss that lasted an eternity, a kiss that sent sweet fire to her every nerve and left her tremulous and unresisting. Taking her hand, he gently led her to the shaggy rug in front of the leaping fire and, saying "Don't move," began undressing her. As his long-fingered, dexterous hands removed each piece of her clothing, he kissed that part of her which was revealed, and when at last she was standing naked in the flickering light, her clothing in a heap at her feet, he stood back and gazed at her with a look that melted her very soul, and said, "You are more beautiful than I could have dreamed."

She stepped forward, but he said, "No, stay there. Let me look at you," and began to undress himself as she stood transfixed in his gaze. When at last he stood unclothed before her, his body honed in shadowed planes by the fire-light, Sidney thought she would collapse with the desire for him, the need of him, the love of him. For she saw that he was beautiful. His body was long and lean, hard, tan, and smooth. It tapered from broad shoulders and chest to narrow hips and long legs, and it gleamed a reddish gold. They stood and hungered for each other, and it struck Sidney that never before had any man looked at her that way, with so much desire, exploring with his eyes every inch, every private place on her body, and it surprised her that she did not feel naked at all. She felt clothed in that look.

He said, "Are you frightened now?" and she whispered, "No," and, sweeping their clothes aside, he sank to his knees in front of her, pulling her down to him, and laid her gently back on the rug. First he kissed her everywhere it was possible to kiss, his strong, gentle hands moving over her, touching her everywhere it was possible to touch, and even moving to places where it seemed impossible to touch, but which turned out to be rapturous and very possible, and every few moments his mouth returned to hers to drink ever more deeply of her. Her hands, too, moved over his body, over the chest, the stomach, the hips, across his back, and she arched up to him, opening like a flower to the golden sunlight of him.

When she had reached what she thought was the brink, sure that at any moment she would go over the edge, he would find somewhere else to kiss and touch and tease and devour, and she would find herself trembling on an even higher plateau of desire and expectation. She heard herself making little whimpering noises, tiny sobs. And then he entered her, and she felt him inside her and part of her, moving in her and with her, and in one long eternity of a moment they held each other tight, tight, tight and went over the long, fiery waterfall together, from exquisite ecstasy down through sweet joy and slowly into gentle exhausted warm comfort.

He looked at her a long time, with a gentle smile, as they lay on the warm shaggy rug, and then he pulled her to him and said, "My Sidney." She burrowed her head into his shoulder and fell asleep in his arms, thinking she would be happy to die right now. For never again, she knew, would she love anyone so much as she loved this man at this moment.

When she woke, the fire was dying and a slight chill was creeping over the room. He slept on. She lay a few minutes in the circle of his arms, trying to remember every detail of what had gone before. She had felt no fear, no shame, nothing but the essential rightness of it. It had been as if they had known each other forever. She looked down at his brown hand, now relaxed but still cupped under her breast, and marveled. He moved a little in his sleep and his grip loosened, and she thought she would try to slip far enough away to reach another log for the fire, but when she moved he was instantly awake. He tightened his arms around her, almost hurting her with his strength, and said, "No. Don't move." He reached one long arm out and tossed a log on the fire, and then kissed her. As the smoking fire began to build up again, so did their passions, more slowly this time, and this time *her* hands began the exploration, and this time she wanted to cry out, "I love you, I love you," but she did not, instead letting herself go in his iron embrace, with visions of fireworks in her head and glory in her heart, into the long, final, shuddering rapture.

CHAPTER NINE

SHE AWOKE AT DAWN. The quilt from the bed was carefully tucked around her, and the fire still blazed, but when she patted the space beside her, there was a terrible emptiness. The dawn was gray and bleak. She rose and with the quilt wrapped around her stood at the window for a long time looking at the ocean, greasy gray and somehow subdued. He had left, she thought, like a thief in the night, not waking her, merely taking his pleasure with her and leaving her to face the chill, leaden morning alone. She thought of packing and leaving—that was what she wanted most to do, but that would be the end of the job, probably the end of her hoped-for career. Not to mention the fact she had turned away so many clients, it would take months to get them back again.

Philip had been right: mixing business and sex was wrong, terribly wrong. So why had he done it? He, not she, had initiated it. She walked to the shower, dropped the quilt, and, making the water as cold as she could stand it, stepped in. She stared out at the dead, leaden ocean under a lowering gray sky and saw that there was no wind, no surf, no white-caps, no long rollers coming to crash on the rocks. The cold water cascaded over her, erasing every trace, every feel of Philip Oliver from her skin. She stood there for a long long time and then, turning off the water, reached for a towel and looked up.

She nearly screamed. He was standing in the room, by the open door, holding two big steaming mugs of coffee and staring at her.

"My God, how long have you been here?" she finally managed, wrapping the towel around herself.

"A few minutes. You looked so wonderful in that shower, against the backdrop of the ocean, that I just wanted to watch you."

He'd changed clothes, she saw, and was wearing gray cords, a white oxford-cloth shirt, and a darker gray crew-neck sweater. He looked, she thought, like a college freshman going to a rush party, except for the definitely mature gleam in his deep green eyes. He must have read something of her earlier thoughts on her face, for he said,

"I'd hoped to be back before you woke. I had to make a phone call." He broke into that devastating grin of his, and her heart melted all over again. He kicked the door shut and handed her a cup of coffee.

"I brought this for protection. I figured if I had one in each hand, I couldn't touch you."

Wrapping the towel more tightly around her, Sidney took the coffee and asked, though she knew the answer, "Why *not* touch me?"

"Because we'd never get out of this room again, that's why. Starvation would set in. And, unfortunately, the others are arriving this afternoon."

But he did touch her, and she him. And then they drank the coffee, which was lukewarm. She put on her own beige cords and a fisherman's sweater and tied her hair back with a bright silk scarf. They went for a long walk, winding up in a canyon through mist-shrouded conifers, some with the palest of green beards of moss on them. They followed a trickle of a stream that tinkled and bubbled down through broken reddish rocks and hummocks of spongy golden grass.

Then, hand in hand, they ran down again, jumping from hummock to hummock, and from side to side of the little stream, laughing like kids. Just before they rounded the clump of twisted black cypress trees that hid the entrance to Timber Cove Inn, they kissed long and deep and then, walking side by side in a dignified manner, went in and ate an enormous breakfast. It was, they agreed, the most beautiful morning they'd ever seen, as they looked out at the smooth silver ocean under a washed white sky.

After breakfast, there was nothing to do but explore the rocky point where the Bufano monument stood, and then clamber down over the rocks, sometimes using handholds and toeholds like mountaineers to get as close to the water as possible.

"I don't understand it," Philip said, perplexed, as he watched Sidney negotiate a particularly difficult outcropping. "You spill your coffee, you miss your bus, but nothing ever happens to you when it's really dangerous."

The rocks had been carved by wind and water into strange and wonderful configurations: there were dark sills of a purple cast, running through pale pink sandstone worn over millions of years into a honeycomb of silver-dollar-sized holes. Other, yellower rocks had been tumbled into knobby piles. Still others were thrust up, dark and jagged, by the movement of the earth's crust, or tossed into the sea to become small islands. The cliff itself dropped almost sheer, two hundred feet, but it had many small caves and narrow ledges and inviting perches to sit on while looking out over the sea. A wind was rising, and the ocean had ceased its subdued heaving and had developed ruffles of whitecaps stretching to the horizon.

Balanced on an outcropping halfway down, with Philip beside her, Sidney said, "Storm coming!"

"Yes," he said, with mock significance, and heedless of their precarious position, he held her tight and kissed her until she was dizzy.

"Stop!" She laughed, trying to pull away. "Someone will see."

"No, they won't. There's nobody here but us mountain goats." But he let her go.

They continued down the cliff face, and at last stood on a narrow strip of damp black sand less than a foot wide.

"Welcome to the sunny beaches of California!" Sidney exclaimed just as the next roller came in and they had to jump for the rocks behind. Even so, they got wet to the knees. After that they waited until each wave had retreated, and in between, dashed from rock to rock, trying to get to the curve of the headland.

"I just want to see what's around the corner," Sidney insisted, as Philip complained, not very hard, about this dangerous business.

Around the corner, it turned out, was Timber Cove itself. A stream, which apparently flowed only in the rainy season, had cut a wedge into the headlands, creating a narrow little semiprotected inlet. It was a mere notch, a tiny nick, one of a very few along the long north coast.

A few waterlogged timbers were scattered around, resting at odd angles on the rocks or wedged between them.

"That's why they call it Timber Cove," Philip explained. "Back in the 1800s, they cut the trees up there on the hills, dragged them down here, and loaded them on ships in the cove. The wood was used to build the houses of San Francisco, I expect."

"How did you learn that?" Sidney asked in surprise.

"I read it in the hotel brochure," he said. "And there are some pictures in the lobby of the contraption they used to get the logs down to the ships. It looked like a medieval drawbridge."

They sat on a rock, out of the wind, and watched the waves rising and the spray starting to fly. Philip said, "This makes the stern and rock-bound coast of New England look like a kiddie playground. No wonder there aren't any small boats out there. There's no shelter anywhere."

"There are harbors at Mendocino and Fort Bragg, farther up," Sidney told him. "But they're tiny. It takes your breath away to watch the fishing trawlers coming in in the evening.

I've watched it. They have to navigate a thirty-foot-wide channel between rocks. It's no wonder this coast has never deveoped. And I hope it stays this way. I love it." There was such conviction in her voice that he turned to her, pulled her close, and buried his face in her hair.

"And I..." he began, but the rest was lost when she lifted her face to his for a kiss. Afterward, she was to wonder for a long time just what it was he would have said had she not stopped him.

It took a long time to find a way back up the cliff face. They stopped at every little cranny for a hug, a kiss, and a laugh. Finally, they walked back to the inn with straight, solemn faces, for the place was beginning to fill up for the weekend, and there were now many more people about. They ate lunch in the dining room, and Sidney felt that everyone in the room should have been staring at them. She felt incandescent. The world was hers. No, not the world, only the best of it, the highest pinnacle of it. And though they only talked about the wind, which was rattling the windows, and the few spatters of rain that had started coming in horizontally, driven by the wind, she could read in his eyes that she *was* incandescent. The light of her in his eyes lit up his whole face, she realized. She dared not look at him too often, though, for fear of bursting out in peals of joyous laughter at the wonderful secret they shared.

A shadow no larger than a fleeting thought came into her mind, and it began to grow and cast a pall over the day. Obviously, this could not go on. They were here for a reason: the discussions. These were scheduled to start tomorrow. Then she would have to sit near him, see him, listen to him, talk to him as if he were just another human being. She could not hang on his every word, look lovingly at his features, reach out and touch him whenever she wanted to. As for that last, she wanted to touch him all the time. Then she brightened. The conference could not last forever, and there would be other days, other times, as sure as ... as sure as what?

Philip must have been thinking along similar lines, for

he said, "Unfortunately, the others will be here later today. And the consultant advises me that South Americans are far more formal than we are, so we'll all be dressing up. Seems a shame, doesn't it, when all you really want to do is take off all your clothes." He leered evilly across the table at her, a look so piratical that only a day ago it would have struck her dumb. Now it made her smile, and she looked around the room to make sure no one had noticed. Apparently no one had. The other diners ate and talked as if nothing were amiss. Just as people not crazed with love always did.

Philip walked her back to her room, staying carefully under the eaves, for now the rain was driving in. The room had been cleaned in their absence, the bed made, the towels replaced, and the fire laid again. Philip lit it. Soon it blazed up, warming the room. The windows facing the ocean were nearly opaque with rain, but nonetheless Philip and Sidney stood looking out at the fury of the storm as if through a hundred tiny distorting lenses. The waves were rolling up and breaking high on the cliff face now, and sometimes a whiff of spray dashed over the top of the headland. Philip held her tight in the circle of his strong arms, and Sidney had never felt so safe, so loved, so secure.

She started to say so, but there was an impatient blare of an automobile horn outside. Philip went over to the front window. Looking down, he said, "Damn. They're here."

"Impatient, aren't they?" Sidney smiled. "Why so heavy on the horn?"

"I guess they want somebody to come out and get the luggage. I can't really blame them." He turned and stopped her before she got to the window. "I've got to go down there and meet them. But before I go . . ." He gathered her to him, holding her so tight that he nearly hurt her, and his mouth came down on hers with such demanding hunger combined with such exquisite sweetness that after a while she feared she might faint with the love and the need of him that flooded her. Her knees buckled, but he caught her, picked her up, and, his mouth never leaving hers, carried her to the bed and laid her down on it. He bent over her, kissing her eyes, her forehead, the tip of her nose, his arms braced in either side of her. Then he straightened.

She groaned.

"I know, I know. Awful, isn't it?" He grinned at her. "Take a nap. You were up very early today, and there will be nothing to do until dinner. See you at five for cocktails."

He went out into the storm, and she lay for a time, thinking about him. Finally, she drifted off into a deep sleep.

CHAPTER TEN

OF COURSE, SHE overslept—no doubt because of all that fresh air and exercise, she thought as she frantically raced around the room gathering her clothes for dinner. It was five-thirty and nobody had wakened her. The room had been cold and dim when she woke, confused as to where she was. When she remembered, she had felt just the slightest annoyance that Philip hadn't come to wake her—and take her to dinner on his arm. Then she realized that that was the last thing he would do. This was a business conference. Besides, she was not really needed for the social preliminaries tonight. She was supercargo, an unnecessary frill. But tomorrow would be different. Then she would be at work.

She slipped into a red-and-black plaid wool skirt, a white blouse with long, full sleeves and a bow at the neck, and plain black pumps. She put gold hoops in her ears and went through her usual struggle with eye makeup. She pinned her hair up, after a fashion, and then stood back and surveyed herself in the mirror. She decided that she had achieved a satisfactory balance between dressing for dinner and dressing for the north coast. Grabbing a raincoat and throwing it over her shoulders, she negotiated the balcony and stairs and without serious water damage entered the lobby at quarter to six.

They were standing in a group around the fireplace: two women, four men, and Philip. They held drinks, talking and laughing. Philip seemed to sense when she entered, for he looked up, over the heads of the people he was talking to, and flashed her his devastating grin. He was wearing a dark suit, a plain white shirt, and a subdued tie. He started forward and then, apparently thinking better of it, bent his dark, elegant head to hear what the woman next to him was saying. However, he moved in such a way as to leave a place beside him for Sidney.

She hung her raincoat on one of the hooks next to the door and made her way across the lobby, past the overstuffed leather chairs and the tanks of tropical fish. As she approached the group, she realized that though she had achieved a balance in her dress, they had tipped over into formality. All the men wore black suits that, although not tuxedos, might well have been from the dapper way they were worn. The two women, she saw, were exactly the opposite physical types—one plump and dark, the other frail and blond— but both were in long gowns and wearing much real-looking jewelry.

There was a lull in the conversation as she took her place next to Philip. The soft music in the background, she realized, was Tchaikovsky's *Romeo and Juliet*. Possibly the most romantic piece of music ever written, she thought. The warmth from the fire seemed to have taken hold in her veins. This was not going to be easy.

Philip put a hand on her shoulder, and her heart raced. But she knew it was only a gesture, a way to bring attention to her so that she might be introduced. He was in control, she thought. This calmed her.

She heard Philip say, "Your Excellency, this is Sidney McKenna, one of my consultants, who will be doing translations for us. Sidney, His Excellency, Gerardo Guillame-Hernandez." The minister of industry of Piedras Negras was a burly man with small, sharp black eyes set in a porcine

face. The eyes fixed themselves on Sidney's bosom and
stayed there, remarkably, while he bent to kiss her hand.
She resisted the temptation to laugh, and she thought she
caught the barest flash of an amused look from Philip's
politely hooded eyes.

"It is a great pleasure to meet you, my dear," said the
minister in almost unaccented but somehow oily English.
"I am sure it will be an even greater pleasure working on
you."

"You mean working *with* me, don't you, Your Excellency?" Sidney said, wresting her hand from his as gently
as she could.

"Yes, of course. That's exactly what I meant." His Excellency put one hand apologetically over his heart. "My
English, you see, is not very good."

Philip Oliver intervened. "On the contrary, it's excellent,
I'd say." Then he subtly eased Sidney away.

"Yuck!" Sidney said under her breath.

"I agree," Philip Oliver replied. Then he raised his voice
and introduced her to three men who looked very much
alike: small, heavily moustached, and wearing tinted glasses.
They were, it seemed, Jaime Flores-Acosta, the minister's
personal aide; Fernando Contreras, a deputy minister; and
Antonio Herrero, a representative from the consulate in San
Francisco.

All murmured over her hand, but none captured it as had
His Excellency.

The lush, dark woman, who was showing generous
cleavage and a diamond and emerald necklace that nearly
made Sidney's mouth drop open, was, it turned out, the
minister's personal secretary. Her name was Eva Mercado.
When Philip introduced her, Sidney could all but hear the
quotation marks around the word *secretary*, and Sidney saw
that Eva was looking her over with none too pleased a look.
She had evidently seen the episode with the minister and,
though she spoke no English, had completely understood
it.

That left the blonde, Alicia Smith. An administrative
assistant with the consulting firm. From New York. She

delivered this information briskly, shaking Sidney's hand. "The boss brought me along for the South American experience. I usually only work the European accounts."

"Where *is* your boss?" asked Philip from behind Sidney.

"He went back to his room for something," Alicia replied. "He said he'd be back in a minute."

"In that case, Sidney, let me get you a drink," Philip said. "What will you have?"

"A Tanqueray martini, please." Philip went off, leaving Sidney face to face with Alicia. She was dressed in what Sidney figured must be the height of current New York chic. Her very low-cut pink dress, made, Sidney realized on closer inspection, of sweat-shirt material, nearly revealed the nipples on her small, flat breasts. Around her neck was a piece of hammered gold shaped exactly like a bookkeeper's eyeshade.

Sidney knew it was incumbent on her to make conversation. "How do you like California?" she asked brightly. "Is this your first trip?"

Alicia's sharp blue eyes and slightly feral features all rose with her plucked brows. "I don't, and yes, it's my first trip," she drawled.

"But if it's your first trip, how do you know you don't like it?" asked Sidney, slightly taken aback.

"I knew I wouldn't like it before I came. As soon as my boss explained that I shouldn't pack my bathing suit, that this wasn't Los Angeles, I knew I'd rather stay in New York. That doesn't mean I won't enjoy being in on these negotiations. This is a big step in my career. The boss says that after this I'll be able to handle anything on my own. Of course, it will have to be in a French-speaking country. I only have my Wellesley French." Switching her tone of voice suddenly, she continued, "Did you go to school?"

Happily, Philip appeared with her drink at that moment, and the disconcerted Sidney was saved from a reply, for Alicia immediately switched her attention to him. Sidney gratefully moved away and stood close to the fire, sipping her drink and listening halfheartedly to the soft Spanish phrases of Jaime Flores-Acosta, the minister's aide, who was talking of the great beauty of the storm outside. No, it was the great beauty of his own country he was talking about, she realized after a while. Bored, she watched Philip, now talking to both Alicia and Eva, who was possessively clutching the elbow of His Excellency, who in turn was casting crafty, sheeplike looks at Sidney. Excusing herself from Jaime Flores-Acosta, Sidney took her drink and walked over to look more closely at the tropical fish, moving away from the heat of the fire to an area where the minister could not see her. She was peering near-sightedly at a yellow-and-white striped fish, a very intelligent-looking fish which had natural horn-rimmed spectacles, when a voice beside her said:

"Sidney? Is that you?"

She swung around and looked directly into the startled pale blue eyes of Max Canning, her ex-husband. She was wrenched back in time four years, all memory of what went between wiped out. He was still boyishly handsome, blond hair falling on his forehead. He still looked like a tennis coach. And he still exuded the dynamic charm that had made her, and others, call him Max the Magician. But then she noticed the lines around his eyes, the too-ruddy cheeks, the heft around his waist, and realized that in four years he had taken on the look of an athlete gone to seed from a little too much of everything. In that same instant she realized that she felt nothing for him. No hate, no love, no emotion at all. She had dreaded this moment all these years, and finally, now that it had happened, she saw him as he really was. And probably always had been.

"Well, aren't you going to say anything?" he persisted.

"How about, 'You're looking well, Max.' Isn't that what they say in the movies, at meetings of this kind?"

"Then I believe my line is, 'What are you doing here?'" he said.

"The same thing you are, I guess. The negotiations. I presume you are Alicia's boss. The consultant from New York?" Sidney smiled sweetly.

He nodded. "And you are . . . ?" he looked at her quizzically.

"The interpreter."

"Who hired you?"

"Pacific Instruments."

"So we're on the same side," he said thoughtfully.

"I thought this was to be negotiations, not war. Interpreters don't take sides."

"I see you still have a lot to learn, my dear ex. A lot."

"I'm sure I have," Sidney said. "So what have you been doing these last four years?"

They talked for a few minutes longer, about their activities and about old friends and acquaintances. Sidney was pleased that their meeting had been carried off in such a civilized manner. Then they went to join the others.

"I see the two of you have met already," Philip said.

"Indeed we have," said Max. "Sidney, in fact, was once a student of mine at Berkeley."

"Oh?" said Philip, a little too flatly.

"We were also married for five years," Sidney stated, even more flatly, and she caught the startled jump in Philip Oliver's eyes.

But at that moment the maître d' touched Philip's elbow to indicate that their table was ready, and in his persona of host, he helped usher them all into the dining room, to a long table set in a corner, giving it an aura of privacy.

Sidney found herself at the end of the table, next to Antonio Herrero from the consulate and across from Eva Mercado. Max was next to Eva, and His Excellency, thankfully, was far down at the other end, next to Philip.

The conversation was not terribly interesting, for Max ignored her, Eva glared at her, and Antonio wanted to talk only of the soccer exploits of his son at St. Ignatius High School. None of this boded well for negotiations, she thought. Here were all these characters, some of them almost caricatures, together in a romantic and isolated hotel in a terrible storm. It seemed more appropriate to an Agatha Christie novel. Perhaps one of the Vietnamese waiters would turn out to be Hercule Poirot in disguise and would tear off his wig, telling them he'd called them all together to tell them the murderer was . . . But there hadn't been a murder. Maybe she ought to wish for one to liven this dinner up. From the glances cast at her, Sidney gathered that, for Eva, she would make a suitable victim.

She plowed through the dinner, not really giving it its due, for it was very good: oysters Rockefeller, fresh local salmon in hollandaise, wild rice, crisp stir-fried snow peas, and several varieties of good Napa Valley wine, along with a green salad and the ubiquitous crusty hot sourdough bread. The waiters hovered, and the conversation continued. Max was talking in halting Spanish to Eva and casting furtive glances down the front of her dress. Sidney almost laughed. He hadn't changed. Alicia, at Philip's elbow, where she had maneuvered herself, was picking at her food. "Tell me, Mr. Oliver, are all you Californians into Scientology?" Sidney heard her say. Sidney suddenly thought of Brice. How he would love hearing about this dinner later.

Then the meal was over, and the storm was still beating at the windows, They all "adjourned," in Max's annoying phrase, to the bar for brandies. After a time, His Excellency begged off, and, taking his aide and secretary with him, went off to his suite. Fernando Contreras and Antonio Herrero wanted to look over some papers before morning, so they drifted off, leaving Max, Alicia, Philip, and Sidney.

"This looks like the home team," Max said. Philip was leaning against a corner of the fireplace, holding his brandy snifter and looking thoughtful, while Alicia, on one of the long leather couches, was edging almost imperceptibly in his direction. Sidney noticed that, without even looking at her, Max reached out a hand and grasped Alicia's wrist, stopping her progress.

"Speaking of teams," Philip said, "can I talk to you, Max and Sidney alone for just a minute?"

"Of course," Max answered. "Off you go, Alicia. We'll call you when you're needed."

Alicia rose, carefully smoothing her dress down to the angles of her body. She stalked off and took the nearest bar stool, pointedly turning her back. Sidney guessed that her ears were probably turned all the way around. Sidney herself was sitting on the edge of the big coffee table, where she could get a better view of Philip. She hadn't had a chance to look at him for at least an hour.

Philip said, "This is a little awkward, but . . . is your, uh, earlier relationship going to interfere with your working together?"

Sidney had given that very subject some serious thought during dinner, but she had reminded herself that her job as interpreter was a neutral one and that no matter what she thought of Max or, for that metter, felt about him, it would not interfere with her ability to translate Spanish into English.

"I don't think so," she said. "I thought about it, and I really don't see why it would."

But Max seemed to disagree. "I'm not so sure. Not that I have any hard feelings at all toward Sidney, none whatsoever. We parted on a note of mutual respect."

Liar, thought Sidney.

"But," Max continued, "do we really need an interpreter here? His Excellency speaks English as well as you or I, and so does Antonio, the one from the consulate. We could prevent any possible problem in, er, communications if we let Sidney work on written translations. We could set up a separate room for her, where she could work by herself, undisturbed."

"No," Philip cut in, frowning. "I want her there, listening."

"Then, no," Max said quickly. "It's certainly no problem with me. None at all."

Sidney excused herself and, remembering to pick up a book from some shelves near the door, made her way back to her room. As she left, she noticed that Alicia had slid back on the couch again and that the three were deep in discussion.

CHAPTER ELEVEN

SIDNEY, WEARING A flannel nightgown, was reading in bed when the tap at the window came. She'd not expected him to come, and after some time spent leaning back on the soft pillows congratulating herself on her successful first encounter with Max, she'd put her glasses on her nose and picked up the book, intending to read herself to sleep. It would keep her from lying there thinking about Philip Oliver's face . . . and body . . . and mouth . . . and hands.

The book was *Two Years Before the Mast* by Richard Henry Dana, and she thought it would be about sailors. It was, but to her surprise it was also about California in the 1830s. She found it quite engrossing. Dana described the bleak and empty coasts, the tiny Spanish settlements, each with a mission and a presidio, where the sailing brig *Pilgrim*, on which he had shipped as a common sailor, had stopped to trade for cattle hides and tallow.

Leafing through, she had found this passage:

The Californians themselves are an idle, thriftless people and can make nothing for themselves. The country abounds in grapes, yet they buy, at a great price, wine

made in Boston. Their fondness for dress is excessive.
The men wear a broad brim hat with a gilt band, a
short jacket of silk, pantaloons open at the sides below
the knee, laced with velveteen, and wear a red sash
around the waist. The women wear spangled satin
shoes, silk gowns, high combs, gilt earrings and neck-
laces. They live in mud huts with dirt floors. For
amusement they have horse racing, bull baiting, cock-
fighting, gambling of all sorts, and fandangoes.

Sidney was chuckling aloud at this when the tap came.
Putting glasses and book down, she ran over to open the
window and heard Philip whispering through the door, "Here.
Hurry up, it's wet out." She glanced at her travel clock and
saw that it was nearly midnight. She fumbled with the lock
and opened the door, and he stepped in. Though he still
had his suit on, his tie was off and hanging from his pocket,
and his collar was unbuttoned. He kissed her quickly, almost
absentmindedly, nearly missing her mouth in his haste, and
grabbed a towel from the pile on the bathroom shelf and
began rubbing his hair. Then she saw that he was soaking
wet.

"What on earth have you been doing?" she said, arms
akimbo in the classic position.

"Climbing out windows. Sneaking around. I'm a thirty-
five-year old adolescent. I haven't done anything like this
since I was a kid in boarding school. I feel like a damn
fool."

"So why did you do it?" she asked innocently.

"Because I can't keep my hands off you," he said, reaching for her.

He held her for a long time, as if he wanted to be sure
of her reality, her solidity. His arms encircling her were
like warm bands of steel, guarding her, protecting her. Then
the feeling slowly changed to an aching need that radiated
through her nightgown and the layers of his clothing that
separated them.

She lifted her face to his, and they kissed, sweetly at

first and then more and more wildly, until they were tearing madly at the clothes, tossing them everywhere. Only much later did Sidney become aware of the hard wooden floor under her shoulder blades and hips and of Philip, lying above her, lifting his eyes from hers and looking at the fireplace. She twisted her head around to see what he was looking at, and they dissolved with laughter at the sight of his jockey shorts smoldering in the ashes.

Afterwards they sat side by side in the bed, he with his arm around her, cradling her. Then his eyes fell on the book. "What are you reading?" he asked.

She showed him the title and read him the passage that had amused her. He laughed in a way that warmed her all over—as if she needed warming. He took the book from her and leafed through it for a moment, and then laughed again. "Listen to this," he said.

"'California is blessed with a climate than which there can be no better in the world, free from all manner of diseases, with forest, fine harbors and rich soil. The Americans are fast filling up the principal towns, and getting the trade into their hands, yet their children are brought up Californians in most respects and if "California Fever" (laziness) spares the first generation, it is likely to attack the second.'" He paused and looked speculatively at her. "I always thought you California natives had hereditary defects."

"Now, now," Sidney countered. "That was a perfect description of Eva. She's not from California."

"I can just picture the minister in velveteen pantaloons." Philip grinned.

"He's pretty awful, isn't he?"

"He's pretty awful, but he's shrewd as hell. Max's dossier on him shows that he's very powerful and has brought several multinationals into Piedras Negras. Their offer is very good: lots of incentives, tax breaks, a skilled labor force, low wages, and a high standard of living. Have you ever been there, by the way?"

"No. Never. My father has, though. It's way up there

in the Andes, dead center in South America, and nobody seems to pay much attention to it. No revolutions, no earthquakes, no wars, and no disasters."

"Must be a very dull country," he murmured into her hair. Bending down, he nipped her lightly on the ear.

"Ouch, you cad," she said, slapping him away. He leaned back against the headboard, and she looked at him sideways. From the corner of her eye she saw the firelight on the broad, finely muscled chest and on his smoothly planed face. His eyes were closed, and there was a faint smile of contentment on his face. His dark hair had dried in rough curls, one of which was dangling over a heavy eyebrow. He opened one eye, looked at her, and grinned, the white teeth flashing in his tanned face. "Like what you see?" he asked.

"Oh, yes," she said weakly. "Oh, yes."

"So do I," he said, looking her up and down, and reaching for her again.

But Sidney was thinking of something else. "You just said that Piedras Negras has low wages and a high standard of living. How is that possible?"

"I dunno. That's what the data say. Per capita GNP is high."

"But," Sidney protested, "per capita GNP doesn't say anything about the spread. There could be ten billionaires and a million starving Indians and you'd get a high per capita income, too."

Philip gave a mock frown: "Cardinal rule number two: never discuss economics in bed." He smiled, Sidney noticed, but he also seemed to withdraw a little. He paused and then said, "But since we're on serious subjects, what about Max?"

That made Sidney move away a little. "What do you mean, what about Max?"

"I mean, how do you feel about him? Can you honestly work with him?"

"I honestly feel nothing about him. I married him when I was young and gullible, and it didn't work out. And now

I'm a different person and so is he, and times are changed, so it's like working with a perfect stranger."

Philip said, "He didn't seem to feel that way. Is he still in love with you?"

"No. Not at all. In fact, I..." Sidney hesitated. "Look, I don't want to talk about it. It won't make any difference. And besides, I've never quizzed you about your ex-wife, have I?"

"No," he said, "and you damn well won't." There was a long, threatening silence, and the sound of the rain slashing against the windows grew very loud in the room. Sidney felt a chill, and she shivered.

After a long time, Philip said softly, "I'm sorry. That wasn't fair at all. It's just that... oh, never mind. Let's just stay off the subject of former spouses." He pulled her close again. "I have some better things to discuss with you, like fandangos."

And again, ignoring the warning bells that were clanging in her mind, equating him and Max, she looked up and said in her most innocent voice: "And what, exactly, is a fandango?"

"The best way to explain it," he said, putting one finger under her chin and turning her face to his, "is to show you."

His lips came down on hers, and his hands began an exploration of her body, gently tracing every line and curve, as if he wanted to memorize the feel of her. He outlined each rounded breast until she could feel it ripening under his touch, moved down the sweet curve of her hip and across her belly, circling, teasing, and then stopped. She found herself on fire, burning with exquisite need. He drew back, and she opened her eyes and saw that he was looking at her with that sexy pirate's grin, and knew that he was waiting for her. She slid down in the bed and pulled him down to her, arching her body against his. But he said, "You're going to have to tell me what you want."

"Touch me," she moaned.

"Where?"

"Everywhere," she whispered, "everywhere."

"There?" he asked.

"Yes, oh, yes."

"And there?"

"Yes, there."

"And here?"

But she could no longer answer him. His hand had at last reached between her thighs, and when he sensed that she could no longer bear it, he rolled her over on top of him and in one fluid motion was inside her.

Then they were no longer two people but one, he moving under her, she over him, pulling his head toward her so that he could kiss her breasts. At last locked together in a burst of passion and fierce joy, they held each other as if the world were coming to an end. As they lay in each other's arms, hearts still pounding and breathing still ragged, he looked her at her with enormous tenderness and said:

"That was a fandango."

When he left in the early dawn, she giggled. His suit, thrown wet over a chair, was ruined, and there was a hint of dark beard on his chin. His rooms, he explained, were clear around on the other side, and he couldn't risk going through the lobby. He had to walk all the way around the inn, on the lee side, avoiding the dining-room windows. He wouldn't scale any windows this time. At least the rain had let up, though the wind hadn't.

"I'm supposed to be a captain of industry." He grinned wryly. "Do captains of industry spend their nights furtively climbing through underbrush in storms, I ask you?"

"Do you want an answer to that?" She said from under the quilts, watching his every beloved move.

"No. Anyway, my love, I can't keep this up. The pace will kill me. See what mixing pleasure with business gets you? It gets you old before your time."

"I thought you were mixing business with pleasure."

"That makes you even older." He came over and kissed her lightly and said, "Sleep well. You've got several hours left. God, it's amazing what a man does to save a lady's reputation." He started out the door.

"Don't forget your own reputation," she called after him.

"Believe me, I'm not. I wonder what it is." He flashed one last, wonderful, tender smile at her and closed the door. She settled down to sleep again, holding the pillow he'd slept on, thinking blissfully how wonderful it was to love and be loved in return. Or could she be sure of that? He'd never actually said he loved her, not in so many words. But he acted as if he did. Was that good enough? For now, yes. For now, she said to herself. The question of Max and the question of Philip's ex-wife were still there, hanging fire. But that could be worked out. Love conquered all. Didn't it?

CHAPTER TWELVE

TIMBER COVE INN had been built with conferences in mind, for there was an enormous room just for that purpose in the southern wing, near the suites of larger rooms where Philip and the minister of industry were staying. Rather than the distracting view of the ocean and the headlands, this room overlooked a tranquil pond with cattails, lily pads, and ferns. A large oval table stood in the middle of the room, comfortable chairs around it. In the corners were smaller arrangements of tables and chairs, conducive to more intimate talks. Some plants and a few pieces of rather nondescript sculpture, not Bufanos, Sidney noticed, stood at various places on tables.

Evidently, Philip and Max had breakfasted early and had been in the conference room poring over papers for a considerable time. Though it was already ten o'clock, they were the only ones there when she arrived. She'd dressed in a beige sweater and skirt and had decided on her loafers, even though she wondered now whether the preppie look was a bit inappropriate. She had brought little else to wear.

Philip, she noticed immediately, looked as if he'd just stepped out of Brooks Brothers. His navy suit was fresh, his blue-and-white striped shirt crisp, and his tie perfectly knotted. But then she noted that his shoes looked a little . ∴. well, damp. She smiled to herself.

Max, on the other hand, looked not only fresh but positively hearty. His suit, too, was perfectly tailored, in a subdued houndstooth check. Like Sidney, he was wearing loafers, but they shouted Gucci, and when he bent over some papers, his open suit jacket gapped to reveal the intertwined YSL monogram on his shirt pocket. He was still extraordinarily handsome, Sidney thought. Still striking in his blondness, still appealing. But she was aware again that the boyish face had grown slightly heavier and that the charm seemed more studied than it once had.

Both men looked up when she entered. "Oh, hi, Sidney" was their simultaneous comment, and then they went back to their conversation. Sidney sat down in a far corner and observed them for a while, the two men in her life, past and present. She decided she much preferred the lean darkness, the subtlety and humor of Philip Oliver to the conventional, hearty, clean-cut blondness of Max Canning. They were both in their mid-thirties, and both were reaching for the top.

But Max would make it bigger. As a faculty member at a leading business school, he had been courted by corporations eager for advice from the academic world. That, in turn, had led to his work with the New York Consulting Group, an organization so respected in the business world that its executives were often hired away at astronomical salaries to run Fortune 500 companies. Max had it made, Sidney thought. And of the two, indeed, it was Max who had the greater ambition. Suddenly the words of a former university dean came to mind: "Max is the kind of guy you want on *your* side." Sidney felt a sudden, uncharacteristic fear for Philip. She hoped the two never locked horns.

Her thoughts were interrupted by the sudden accession of His Excellency and his entourage, who had breakfasted late together and now swept in, en masse. All were dressed in dark suits and white shirts, including the plump Eva, who had put on a very secretarial-looking outfit with a huge

white jabot, reminding Sidney of her own "banker's suit."
Eva was also wearing enormous dangling diamond earrings
and carried a steno pad and pencil. Philip and Max stood
when the group entered, and there was an exchange of
greetings and a general fuss about seating. Max asked Sidney (or, more accurately, told her) to go get Alicia, wherever
she was. "I'm not your gofer" Sidney nearly remarked, but
thought better of it, and went out and found Alicia dressed
Montgomery Street style, drinking coffee, and ostenta-
tiously reading the *Wall Street Journal*. She looked, Sidney
thought, as if she were posing for an ad for a bank.

When they returned, it was decided that Alicia, who
knew shorthand, would take notes. So would Eva, of course.
Not word-for-word notes, but the general gist of the discussions, which would be in English. Sidney would be
called upon for emergencies, to iron out linguistic difficul-
ties, or to provide the most accurate phrasing when needed.

Philip led off with a short, neat speech. To this, Max
added a few words. All the while Eva, who didn't understand English, took voluminous notes.

Then His Excellency replied, outlining the desires of his
country in this most interesting matter. He said, "I am au-
thorized to" twenty-three times, Sidney counted. He occasionally snapped his fingers at Jaime, Fernando, and
Antonio, and one or the other would slide a paper across
the table, and from it he would pull another statistic.

Exactly an hour later, Eva suddenly said, in Spanish,
"Mother of God, but this is boring!" and flounced out the
door without another word. His Excellency continued without missing a beat, but suppressed smiles passed between
the Americans in the room. Eva was quite right, Sidney
thought. She herself had read it all while translating. She
stopped listening and gazed at Philip Oliver. He was managing well, displaying a look of polite interest. Once or
twice Sidney caught his eye, and there would be a flash of
humor for the barest of instants before he looked blandly
away. And there were other times when she hadn't been
looking at him but could suddenly feel his eyes on her. She
was, she thought, bearing up rather well, her behavior im-

peccably professional. But then, His Excellency's rhetoric was enough to douse the merest spark of emotion.

His Excellency switched from a litany of figures to his analysis of the stability of the government of Piedras Negras, and Sidney perked up a little. She had been wondering about the blank she had drawn on this country. Piedras Negras was not much in the news. "No labor unions," the minister was saying, "a docile work force." The same president, he noted, was voted back into office every six years by an overwhelming majority of the people. A well-educated work force it was, too, he continued, but not too well educated. Too much education made for unrest.

"My government does not lure foreign capital into our country only to nationalize it, as others have done," said His Excellency. "As American capitalists, you can appreciate that." Sidney visualized Philip suddenly as the bloated plutocrat out of a Thomas Nast cartoon. It didn't work. Max fit that picture better.

"The cost of democracy can be high, the cost of a strong, popular, anti-Marxist government," said His Excellency. "Defense costs alone . . ." Sidney saw that Max was nodding encouragement, but Philip frowned slightly. The minister's words were putting her on edge. Visions of gaunt, hungry Indian faces leaped into her mind.

His Excellency ran down just before lunchtime. A two-hour break was agreed on, and everyone stretched and moved out to lunch. Sidney ate alone, her only option for company being Eva, who disappeared pointedly before Sidney could ask. Philip, Max, Alicia, and His Excellency sat at a table for four, and the three aides were nowhere to be seen. Sidney went for a walk on the cliffs and finally, with time still to spare, sat in the lobby reading *Two Years Before the Mast*. At two, everyone filed back into the conference room—except Eva, who had still not returned.

The speeches over, now they would get down to the "nitty gritty," as Max put it. At last, Sidney was able to put her Spanish to use. There were, it seemed, a few words for which His Excellency didn't know the Spanish equivalents: *constraints, learning curve,* and, surprisingly, *bottom line.*

They discussed the basics: tax advantages, what percentage of equity would be locally owned, what proportion of the management would be American, whether housing for the workers would be provided. Sidney had to admit that Max was good, very good at what he did. She guessed he'd been to Piedras Negras; she was impressed with his knowledge. Even Alicia, she noted grudgingly, had brought out some sharp points. It was evident that they were moving toward agreement, but it was equally obvious that much more remained for discussion.

By late afternoon, everyone was looking a bit wan, satiated with facts and figures. Even Philip had taken off his coat and loosened his tie. Only the minister still seemed his usual florid, hard-driving self. They all agreed to break until morning, and as they filed out the door, Sidney felt a pinch and found His Excellency breathing heavily behind her. Then she wished she hadn't worn her loafers. She would have loved to grind a spike heel into his instep.

After dinner, Philip called a strategy meeting in his suite near the conference room. Sidney was not invited. She told herself that this was only to be expected—her role as translator did not require that she be present—but she was a little disappointed nevertheless.

Bored, she spent an hour or so idly watching the fire in the enormous fireplace and chatting with the minister's aide, Jaime. Eva and His Excellency himself had retreated to their rooms. Jaime told Sidney a great deal about Piedras Negras, delivering much the same spiel his boss had earlier that afternoon. There was a nagging doubt that kept rising in Sidney's mind, one that couldn't quite be shaken off. Occasionally something Jaime said would ring a small bell that something was wrong, out of kilter, but she could never quite put it into words. If anything was wrong, she was thinking, it was certainly none of her business. And, after all, what did she know about opening up an assembly plant in a country she'd barely heard of?

She struggled with herself for a while, then put it out of her mind. Half of her listened to Jaime, and the other half thought happily about what she and Philip would do after the conference. She'd show him the Marin headlands, Point Reyes, Angel Island. She dreamed and drifted. But then Jaime's voice penetrated her consciousness.

". . . dealing with Cimax Corporation. Unfortunately, the copper all turned out to be on the Chilean side. But then it turned out that there was molybdenum. . . ."

Sidney sat up straight. Cimax was the corporation her father worked for, and suddenly the nagging doubt turned into a certainty. A few years ago, her father had spent about six months in Piedras Negras. She stood suddenly and looked about the lobby. There had to be a telephone here someplace; Philip had used it. At last, she spotted a pay phone on the wall by the door.

"Oh, excuse me, Jaime," she said, recollecting herself. She smiled politely at his look of surprise. "Something you said just reminded me, I've got to call home." Jaime would assume she meant San Francisco. He rose politely and bowed. "I shall await your return," he said.

Sidney realized she could never come up with enough change for a phone call to Peru, and she did not want to call from the exposed pay phone anyway. However, as she approached, she saw that behind the reception desk was the manager's office, which offered both privacy and a telephone. The manager himself was standing at the bar, talking with some of his guests. He was only too pleased to let her use his private office. She would bill everything to her home phone, she promised him.

She went in, but being out of sight of the main part of the lobby, she didn't close the door. It would be, she estimated, about midnight in Lima. She'd wake everyone, but if she waited until morning, her father would be at work and she could not call him there.

The call went through like lightning, reminding Sidney of the old days before communications satellites, when one went on a waiting list for the cable and *might* be lucky enough to receive an appointment twenty-four hours later.

Her father answered. He had not been asleep after all. They exchanged pleasantries, but quickly. Both knew that such calls cost four dollars a minute.

"Dad," Sidney said, "what do you know about Gerardo Guillame-Hernandez?"

"Enough to know that we wouldn't deal with him."

"Why not?"

"Piedras Negras is a military dictatorship. He's the one civilian in government, and the most powerful man in the country. Also the richest. He's a breed that has died out in a lot of countries down here. He likes very big bribes. They're usually wrapped up so neatly in the financial figures that it takes a real expert to figure them out, but you can be sure that at least half of any foreign investment made there will end up in his pocket."

"Or his Swiss bank account?" Sidney asked.

"That, and art works and American real estate and gold," her father said. "Another thing I don't like about Piedras Negras: it's a poor, miserable little country and the government is doing nothing to make it better. The attitude is 'Take the money and run.' Those generals are not nice people."

"Dad, do you think anything's changed since you were there?"

"I doubt it. Nothing ever does in those countries. Until they have one helluva revolution."

Sidney looked up as her father spoke and saw a figure standing in the doorway. It was Max, and he was smiling benignly.

"Uh, I've got to go," Sidney said swiftly into the phone. She didn't want Max to know what she was doing. "I'll be seeing you soon," she added.

"Wonderful," said her father. "Then you can tell me what this phone call was all about." Then, parentlike, he added, "Sidney, are you okay? Do you need money or anything?"

For once, Sidney was not fibbing in the slightest when she said, "No, but thanks anyway. I'm fine, really fine."

When she hung up, Max was still there.

"Just wanted to use the phone," he said, but it was clear

he had been listening, she thought, her heart sinking. Perhaps for quite a while.

"I just wanted to find out how my cats were doing," Sidney said, and immediately wished she had said nothing. Now she was in the position of having lied. Not that lying made much difference to Max, but it did to her. She had not meant for the phone call to be deceitful, but Max's presence somehow made her feel it had been.

"Is the meeting over?" she asked quickly.

Max nodded. "Everyone's ready to drop," he said.

There was no tap on her door that night. She undressed, brushed her hair out, and then sat in bed, in the firelight, watching the moonlit ocean. She felt very alone. If this was the big league, she didn't like it. Max surely knew what he was doing. But did Philip? She didn't want to know the answer.

The next morning, which dawned bright and sunny, Eva livened things up at breakfast by insisting that she be taken back to San Francisco. She had, she pointed out, been told she was coming to the United States on a working vacation. To her, work was shopping, and there was no place to shop within a hundred kilometers of this deserted, miserable place. Antonio, the man from the consulate, was dispatched to return with her. A few frantic phone calls ascertained that there was a suite available at the hotel nearest Tiffany's. The big black Mercedes from the consulate wheeled around, spraying gravel, heading for the highway. Eva, Sidney noticed, had not forgotten to cast her one last murderous glare of warning, just before the woman was handed into the back seat by His Excellency.

The morning session revolved around finance. Max in particular kept bringing up the subject of "foreign exchange exposure." Sidney did not have to translate that for His Excellency. And she, too, knew what it meant. If Piedras Negras devalued its money, any investment made there in American dollars would lose much of its value. As she translated the phrase *downside risk* into Spanish, she appreciated her M.B.A. training—truly—for the first time. For this sort of work, it was invaluable. The discussion continued, with Max in particular talking of covers and hedges and currency futures. This was, Sidney knew, complicated stuff. She looked at Philip. He was listening intently.

But when lunchtime arrived, Philip said, "I think we need to discuss this among ourselves this afternoon, Your Excellency. May we resume all this in the morning?"

His Excellency was reluctant and argued for an evening resumption. It was agreed on. Sidney ate lunch alone once again. Philip, Max, and Alicia retreated to Philip's suite after lunch and did not come out. Sidney went for another walk along the headlands and decided she could bear it no longer. She had to tell Philip what she had learned from her father. She walked back to the door of Philip's suite. She stood a moment before knocking.

To her chagrin, Max opened the door.

"Yes?"

"I've got to talk to Mr. Oliver. Alone. It's important."

She peered over his shoulder into the room but could not see Philip.

"Sidney, we're really busy. Can't it wait?"

"No, Max, it can't."

"Are you ill?"

"No, of course not," Sidney said in disgust.

Then Philip's voice floated out of the room. "Sidney, give us five minutes, and then you can come in."

She had to agree. In the intervening time, she went and got a mug of coffee from the warmer by the bar. When Max opened the door, she was leaning against the frame, holding her coffee and tapping her foot. Max frowned at her as he and Alicia left, but she stepped quickly into the room. She had closed the door behind her before he could say anything at all.

The suite was much larger than Sidney's room and had an even more stunning view of the rocky promontory and the Bufano statue. It had, she noticed, a copper-lined hot tub, as well as far less rustic furnishings. It also contained a couch and a large table, over which were spread what seemed to be hundreds of pieces of paper. Philip was standing by the window, his coat jacket off, his vest unbuttoned, and his tie loosened. The light was behind him, and Sidney could not make out the expression on his face. The sun was streaming in the window and directly into her eyes.

"May I sit down?" she finally ventured into the silence.

"By all means," came the reply, and she maneuvered her way to the chair closest to the window. She wanted him in the sunlight where she could read his expression. She felt no warmth coming from him at all.

He sat down opposite her, and when she met his eyes, she saw he was looking at her with the same polite interest with which he had listened to the minister. Her heart sank, but she said, "There's something I have to tell you."

"I thought as much," he said coldly.

"I made a phone call last night—" she began, but he cut her off.

"I know about it."

It had been Max, of course, who told him, Sidney knew. But she was not to be sidetracked. She plunged on. "That man, Guillame, is a crook."

"He's also a goon," Philip replied flatly.

"Then, don't you see, you mustn't deal with him."

He looked at her intently for a moment and there was a flash of anger in his eyes. Slowly, he said, "Sidney, that is absolutely none of your business. You forget what your job is supposed to be. Translation. You are not an expert on international business. Or character analysis, for that matter.

"I know that! But I do know right and wrong when I see it." Her mind was racing. Didn't he care about what was right and wrong? Was he another Max?

He said, his face stony, "Frankly, I don't want you mixed up in this at all. It was a mistake, involving you."

"Please listen!" she said desperately. "Max has absolutely no scruples. I know him better than you do. He'll lead you astray. You'll be bribing people, keeping double sets of books. Are you prepared to go that far to save Pacific Instruments?"

His eyes narrowed and his lips became a thin line. "Sidney, I want you out of here. Now. Go back to San Francisco. Your job here is over."

Torn between fury at his refusal to listen to her and her sickening realization that his beloved company meant more to him than decency and ethics, Sidney could think of nothing to say. She stared at him, feeling the blood draining from her face. With effort she stood up, gathering her resolve.

"Then I'm leaving." she snapped. "But you owe me some money."

"I'll have your check mailed."

"No, I want it now."

"I'll have to write you a personal check."

"That's fine," she said, and told him the amount to the penny.

While he hunted down his checkbook and wrote out the check, Sidney paced the room, passing the table on which the papers were scattered. Something caught her eye there, something familiar. She looked more closely. Even without her glasses she could tell that it was the item from the society column about their dinner at Ernie's. With it were two more clippings. By squinting, she could barely make them out.

"The elusive Mr. Chips has emerged from Silicon Valley," it read. "Our spies tell us he's been to all the in places, including taking in Peter Mintun, with a lovely local who claims it's 'something very big.' Her name? Sidney McKenna. Old timers fondly remember her grandfather, James McKenna, who was on the Ess Eff Pee Dee for forty years."

The third clipping was on green paper, so that Sidney knew it was from the Business Section. It was longer, and it began: "Pacific Instruments has booked most of secluded Timber Cove Inn, on the Sonoma Coast, along with the New York Consulting Group, for a . . ." But before she could puzzle out any more, Philip was handing her a check.

"Interesting reading, isn't it?" he said.

"Where did you get them?" she asked.

"Max has a clipping service. I saw them for the first time last night."

"I suppose Max told you I planted them?"

"He suggested it as a possibility."

"And do you believe him?"

"Did you plant them?"

Sidney turned on her heel. Reaching the door, she spun back and threw him an icy glare. "That question is beneath contempt," she snapped. As she slammed out the door, she heard him say, "Don't forget to tear up your copy of the contract."

CHAPTER THIRTEEN

SIDNEY REMEMBERED LITTLE about the long drive back to San Francisco, at least until she saw the side road that led off to the right, just before the approach to the Golden Gate Bridge. She was driving fast, coming down the long grade to the bridge, and she had to stand on the brakes to make the stop sign at the abrupt end of the short freeway exit. As the little Volkswagen ground its way up the steep, unpaved road, past abandoned artillery emplacements from as far back as the Civil War, Sidney realized she'd been lucky. The Bug wouldn't go much over fifty, unless it was downhill. Had she been in some other car, back on the Freeway, she'd probably have wrapped it and herself around a tree, at 120 miles an hour. Her only thought had been to get back to San Francisco, fast.

She drove carefully now, peering ahead only at the road for her favorite turnout. She was on the Marin headlands, opposite the city, and she remembered ironically that she'd wanted to bring Philip Oliver here. Well, he'd never know what he was missing, she thought as she stopped the car's snub nose against the log that formed the only barrier to a

500-foot drop. It was late afternoon, still sunny, and for once the wind wasn't howling at gale force. She got out and sat on one of the benches at the verge of the cliff.

At her feet, the ground dropped away almost vertically, grassy hillside plunging down into the sea, fringed by black rocks and white surf. Below her, cutting across the brilliant blue bay, was the collosal red span of the bridge, its double cables forming graceful parabolas between its twin towers. She could see matchhead-sized cars speeding along its deck. In the bay itself were green, wooded Angel Island and rocky little Alcatraz, its lighthouse flashing even in daylight. Dozens of sailboats skittered on the water, freighters and tankers with their tugboat escorts sliding relentlessly past them. And beyond the bridge floated the white crystal City. From the tongues of the wharves extending into the bay, San Francisco was stacked higher and higher on its hills, culminating in the downtown skyline, whose silhouette was made unique by the pyramidal Transamerica Tower.

No wonder, Sidney thought, that writers from Mark Twain on could only describe this city in terms of Persian gardens, of Taj Mahals, of the thousand and one nights of Scheherazade. "Baghdad by the Bay," they'd called it. There were no words, not in any language she knew, to describe it.

And, as always, it raised her spirits. Some. There was no place for them to go but up, after all. Sidney had to hand it to Philip Oliver, all right. He was right about a lot of things, especially his cardinal rules. Fishing off the company pier, as he had so nicely put it. It got you nothing but old, very fast. But he'd broken his own rule—and looked to be planning to break quite a few others. He was just like Max. What a pair they made! Butch Cassidy and the Sundance Kid!

It had taken her quite a while to see through Max. But not as long to see through Philip. Still too long, though. How could she have been so deluded? She'd imagined herself the love of his life. He'd never said anything about it, never even said he loved her. But he let her think it, because he knew it was the way to break down her defenses. But then, again, maybe she'd dreamed it all up herself. Probably. Blind fool! Idiot!

Sidney looked around furtively to be sure she was alone. She walked over to her car and gave the door on the driver's side a hearty kick, being careful not to hurt her toes. There! But the door was already so battered that the resulting dent was not very visible and therefore not at all satisfying.

Well, anyway, she thought, walking back to the bench, she'd show him. She'd become an international consultant and she'd show him. He'd be begging for her advice—her *ethical* advice.

No, he wouldn't. Nobody would. She'd been fired!

Fired! That meant no referrals, no foothold in Silicon Valley, no helping hands up the long ladder. And what a wonderful way to get rid of a bed partner who'd become a nuisance—fire her!

Realistically, though, it did present a problem. She'd have to build her business back up. She thought again of all the contracts she'd lost over the last month. She'd allowed herself to become too tied up with Pacific Instruments, too caught up in what it seemed to offer. Just to add insult to injury. Or heedlessness to stupidity. All Philip Oliver cared about was his money and a roll in the hay. In that order.

Positive thinking. That was the answer. How could she put all this in a positive context? Well, she'd learned a lot. A learning experience, that was it. With a month lost out of her life. And lost pride. No, don't think that way. Just be glad you caught on before it was too late, she told herself. But maybe it was already too late. Think positive, Sidney. Think: bastard, skunk, wimp, creep!

Sitting there staring out at the City, Sidney barely noticed the small black car that crept up to the turnout. Dusk was on the western horizon and there was a chill in the air. The fog was approaching, though still out to sea. But she did notice the two teenagers when they got out of the car. He was Chinese and she was Latin, and both were dressed in jeans and parkas, lumpy unisex style. Sidney watched warily as the boy seated the girl on a bench and then returned to the car to pull out a large black cassette player and a Styrofoam cooler.

Oh, great, Sidney thought. Just what I need. Beer drinking, can throwing, screaming rockers, up here. If he turns that thing on, I'm going to knock it in the bay. I don't care if he *does* belong to a motorcycle gang.

The boy returned to the bench and opened the cooler. He pulled out a bottle of champagne and two stemmed glasses, and with infinite care peeled off the gold paper and eased the cork out. There was a sharp pop, and he put down the bottle and climbed a little way down over the edge of the cliff. Sidney realized, in some awe, that he was retrieving the cork. He put cork and paper neatly back into the cooler, poured two glasses of champagne, and handed one to the girl.

By now the entire vast panorama, with the City as its centerpiece, had assumed a chalky, pinkish glow from the setting sun. The last lagging small boats were setting for home, and the fog had reached the deck of the bridge, though the two red towers rode above it. There was a bluish haze over the surface of the bay and the wharves. A few lights were coming on, one by one, in the high rises and along the water. Then, somewhere, Sidney imagined, someone threw a switch, and the street lights of San Francisco came on, their grid pattern running up and down the hills.

It was just then that the boy got the cassette player going. Softly came the tones of a slow, poignant rock ballad she'd heard many times—"When the Lights Go Down in the City."

The boy and the girl toasted each other and kissed lightly. Then they sipped their champagne and watched the lights blink on, one by one, across the bay.

Sidney got into her car and drove down the hill, blinking back the tears.

It was somewhere between the north and south towers of the bridge that she made the decision to go to Peru. She raced to her house and headed for the telephone to see if she could get on the next plane out. She could, and the connecting flight left at four the next day. She called Dolores and told her she was going to visit her parents, with no further explanation. Brice agreed to keep the cats while she was gone, but protested quite a lot when she wouldn't explain her sudden change of plans.

He said, "Is somebody sick down there?"

"No, I'll explain when I get back."

"But the thing at Timber Cove Inn. What happened?"

"Brice, I really can't talk about it."

"Okay, but why are you going to Peru?"

"Because I have some money, I haven't seen my parents in a long time, and I need a vacation. Now, stop asking me!"

She spent the evening repacking, slept a few hours, and the next morning walked to her branch bank to cash Philip Oliver's check. She darted back to the house, cleaned out the refrigerator, and put everything that might spoil into Brice's, with a note: "Don't forget to water my plants and to forward *bills only*." She tried to think of an appropriate message for her answering machine, failed, and decided to unplug both machine and telephone. She showered, dressed, and then remembered that she hadn't told her parents she was coming. She plugged the phone back in and made the call. They were surprised but pleased and would meet her at the airport.

She put on her makeup, ate a can of soup, washed the pan, bowl, and spoon, and left them in the dish drainer. She unplugged the phone again. She gave the cats a good brushing, which they liked, and a big hug, which they didn't. She decided she was rich enough to take a taxi to the Airporter bus terminal, so she wouldn't have to wrestle two suitcases onto a Muni bus. She plugged the phone back in again and called a cab. She unplugged the phone.

She took the cab to the Airporter terminal and the Airporter to the airport, arriving just in time to pick up her tickets. She checked her baggage all the way through to

Lima and bought a paperback to read on the plane. At the last minute she remembered her Operations Research course, got to a pay telephone, and miraculously found the professor in his office. She explained that she was going out of town on an emergency and didn't know when she would be back. He said he'd give her an Incomplete for the course.

She was one of the last to board the plane and ended up in the smoking section. No food was served on the one-hour flight, but she had a drink and felt giddy as she waited in the enormously congested Los Angeles International Airport, which for some strange reason was abbreviated "LAX" on the baggage tickets. She boarded her flight to Peru at six, downed with surprising relish an entire meal of plastic airline food, and slept most of the way to Lima. From decision to arrival, less than thirty-six hours had passed.

Her father was standing behind a wooden barrier outside the tin-roofed customs shed when Sidney came out. Buffeted by the swarming crowd, she stopped for a moment, looking at him, before he caught sight of her. She saw a few more lines in the craggy, weathered face and noticed that his hair was now an iron gray. Her heart skipped a small beat as the realization that her father, her rock of Gibralter, was mortal, struck her for the first time. But then he spotted her and she saw that his blue eyes—the clear blue eyes of a sky at morning, just like hers—were as young as ever.

She dropped her two suitcases and ran to him, hugging him with all her strength, right over the barrier. He returned the hug, laughing, and in that moment Sidney knew that nothing ever changed between them. There was a commotion behind her, and Sidney remembered her suitcases. She retrieved them and got an impolite glare from an American businessman who had nearly tripped over them.

Summer was coming on in Lima, and the squalid smog that hung over the city all winter had disappeared with the sea breezes. Sidney's father took the superhighway into town, threading the car through an endless stream of battered taxis, black Mercedeses, and dilapidated buses.

As they passed the ancient ornate cathedral and the wide avenues and the stolid gray German-style government buildings, next to a barrio of squatter shanties made of old wood scraps, old Coca-Cola signs, and pieces of tar paper, Sidney knew she was in South America again. It, like her father, would grow a little older, but it would never change.

Her parents' house was in the pleasant Miraflores section of the city, Spanish-colonial-style white stucco and red tile, behind a high wall. The guard at the gate threw it open, and Sidney saw her mother.

Sidney was out of the car and into the house almost before the car had stopped. Her mother came forward, and as they hugged, Sidney saw, over her mother's shoulder, the silver-framed wedding picture standing on the big black grand piano. Her mother, unlike Lima and her father, would never grow older. She was still the black-haired Eurasian beauty who had married the handsome Irish football hero the day they both graduated from Stanford. Only now, her mother was dressed in designer jeans and a silk blouse, not the antique lace of the picture.

"Don't ask," Sidney said. "I'll tell you and Dad all about it later. I just want to spend some time with you both."

As always, Sidney was grateful for her parent's nonintervention. They never pressed her or invaded her privacy, and they didn't now. They seemed to accept her sudden appearance, taking it all in the relaxed fashion that characterized them. Within a day or so, Sidney had caught up on all the family news and had fallen into a pleasant rut. She found an Indian hammock, bought as a souvenir on some long-forgotten trip, and rigged it between two of the carefully nurtured trees in the immaculately kept garden. She proceeded to read, sleep, and drink *limonada* in this hammock for a week. Finally it dawned on her that her behavior was peculiar, if not loutish, and she got out of the hammock, got dressed, and hauled her mother on a tour of the museums.

Finally satiated with Inca gold and pre-Columbian art, she talked her father into taking a few days off and going to Lake Titicaca, where they rented a boat and went trout fishing. Her father, acclimated to the 12,000-foot altitude, enjoyed it thoroughly. Sidney suffered from altitude sickness and got a ferocious headache. She caught nothing.

Upon their return to Lima, she found that there was mail for her. She opened the largest piece, a manila envelope, and several bills fell out. There was also a letter enclosed:

Dear Sidney,

Hope you are having a great time in Lima, whatever it is you are doing.

Your car has been ticketed three times. I couldn't move it because you took the keys with you. There was another storm a week ago, and there are asbestos shingles from your roof all over the neighborhood. I picked up as many as I could. No damage inside the house, though. Its going to be a bad winter, they say. Other than that, your place is fine, except for the rhododendron in front, which seems to have died or something.

You might be interested to learn that the Pacific Instruments stock issue has been *the* subject of conversation around here. It even made the national news. It came out at $10 a share and by noon had gone to over $100. It seems that they announced the week before that they had the inside track on some new "laser process for gallium arsenide devices." That doesn't mean a thing to me (does it to you?), but apparently it did to the seething masses out there who like to take flyers on companies that have all that high-tech-sounding stuff. Naturally, the stock dropped back down again the next day, but the papers had a field day with stories about instant millionaires.

Or maybe you knew all about it anyway. You never told me one thing about the work you did for Mr. Chips. Have you retired down there on your ill-gotten gains? I assume you bought a few of those stocks yourself, based on inside information. Don't forget

the pre-Columbian statue you would have promised
me if you had thought about it.

Love,
Brice

P.S. You missed Pavarotti. Opera in the Park was last
Sunday.

There was another letter, on Jarndyce, Cooley, and Alexander stationery:

Dear Sidney,
    We've missed your cheerful face around here. When
are you coming back? Dolores says to tell you that
she waits with bated breath to hear your adventures.
    It would be a great help to know when you are
coming back, because several clients of mine are in
need of your services. I gave them your phone number, but unless you get back pretty soon, they're going
to have to find someone else.
    The Forty-niners have won two in a row.
    Regards to your parents. I've always enjoyed seeing
them when they were here.

Jock

JKE/bf
Enc. 1

"Enc. 1" was an invitation to a cocktail party at the
Eddys'. The date was nearly two weeks away. Underneath
the specifics of time and place, Dolores had written: "Duty
calls. This is one of those things for Jock's partners and
clients. Please come and liven things up. Bring anyone you
like. D."
    These letters gave Sidney the sudden realization that life
did not stop when one ran away from it. In fact, it seemed
as if, when you weren't looking, it speeded up. So she sat

down with her parents and told them the whole grisly story, somewhat expurgated, and when she was through, realized that she had Philip Oliver out of her system. She could go back and slip right into her old life without the slightest effort. The same old problems, the ones she knew how to cope with, were right there waiting for her. She had even missed them. She had missed San Francisco and Brice and Jock and Dolores and the cats and the car and the roof and the grandfather clock and her work and even her Operations Research course.

It had been a close call, she explained to her patient mother, who, on the final day of Sidney's visit, had joined her in the garden. But he was another Max, Sidney went on, a wolf in pirate's clothing. She was better off without him. Her mother merely smiled. Her father appeared, with more offers of money, but Sidney told them she didn't need it. Indeed, she had a lot left. And there was only one more year to go in school. Then her degree would be the key to the job she wanted. No more of this back-door stuff. She loved languages, but the stint at Timber Cove had taught her that they weren't enough. What had Philip said to her? *I hired you to translate, nothing more?*

Jock and Dolores's party had seemed an excellent reentry point, so Sidney had timed her return to fall on the day before. Brice met her at the airport, and she gave him a sketchy account of what had happened. ("Fired?" he said. "You got *fired?*") He in turn caught her up on what had gone on in her absence. The 49ers were on a winning streak, and the town was starting to get a little crazy. Park and Rec, having been defeated on its first traffic diversion plan, was working on another, worse one. There had been a small earthquake two days before, but no damage. Brice's sister and her husband and their two kids had been through town on a short visit. He liked them, but . . .

In the intervening day between her arrival and the party, Sidney restocked her house with food, mailed off checks to pay bills, and made a few phone calls to let clients know she was back in town. She talked to the cats, and they seemed almost to recognize her. She saw that the smaller one, Harrison, had chewed off the backs of three books in her absence: that was his revenge for her desertion. She checked the rhododendron and found that it was not "or something"; it was dead. She called the roofer. Finally, she decided that it might be worth a trip down to the Hall of Justice to protest the parking tickets.

CHAPTER FOURTEEN

JOCK USHERED HER in the door, saying "Welcome back."
They hugged warmly. The party was in full swing, and the
condo was crowded. Sidney recognized a few faces that she
was able to put names to and a few that she was not, but
most were strangers.

"Where's Dolores?" Sidney asked.

"In the kitchen, I think. With the caterers," Jock replied.
Just then Dolores appeared and, seeing Sidney, made her
way through the crush. She looked splendid in a floor-length
black velvet dress with a pink sash. Sidney, watching her,
felt suddenly short and frowsy in her green silk blouse and
matching wool skirt. She could never in a million years
look as regal as Dolores.

"For heaven's sake, Jock," Dolores said. "Take Sidney's
coat." But she hugged Sidney before he could help her off
with it. Finally, Sidney struggled out of the coat, handing
it to Jock, who disappeared with it to the bedroom.

"Come back to the kitchen with me," Dolores was saying.
"I've got to help the caterer get the oven working. Now tell
me all about it." They were working their way through the
crowd.

"All about what?"

"Peru. The Pacific Instruments job. Everything. You've got a lot of explaining to do. Things have really been popping since you left."

"What things?" Sidney said disingenuously.

"For one thing, Philip Oliver's been all over the newspapers. Or his company has." Dolores was putting trays of hors d'oeuvres in the oven and fiddling with dials on the stove.

"So I heard."

"Darn it. I can't get this thing to work," Dolores muttered. "I wish I'd bought that microwave. I'm going to have to get Jock to try to fix this. Come on. There's somebody who wants to meet you. A nice young lawyer who just came in with the firm."

"Does he want any translating done?" Sidney asked.

"Not that I know of, but he's new in town and has a sailboat."

"Sorry, Dolores, I don't think I'm really interested, at least not right now. I've got plenty of work to catch up on."

But Dolores dragged Sidney, protesting a little, into the living room and pointedly introduced her to a pleasant-looking man with crinkly eyes and an accent Sidney recognized as Philadelphian.

"Jim, this is Sidney. Introduce her around, will you? I've got to find Jock."

Jim, who of course turned out to be the sailboat owner, seemed happy to oblige, and Sidney soon found herself caught up in the swirl of conversation. She had feared that the talk would be legalese, and there was some of that, but mostly it centered on the "Big Game"—the annual Cal-Stanford football game, which was coming up that weekend. While the elegantly dressed wives rolled their eyes heavenward, grown men, some of them in their seventies relived their college rivalries. Sidney noticed that Jim was casting admiring glances at her, and replied politely to his questions. She admitted that she was a U.C. Berkeley graduate. She hated to admit that she had never been to a U.C. game, much less the Big Game. She tried to explain how a whole city could get wrapped up in a college game. While she was telling this to him in an undertone, the talk around them continued.

"Do you have something like that in Philadelphia?" Sidney asked politely. He started to answer and then stopped. One of the men in the group in which they were standing was saying, "Well, I don't expect to be around for the Big One. I don't expect to live that long." Another answered, "Don't count on it. They say it's coming in the next few years."

Jim looked puzzled. "I thought that the Big One was next Sunday."

Sidney said, startled, "How do you know that?"

"They were just talking about it." Jim nodded toward the small circle of people, which they had now drifted away from.

"But," Sidney said, "nobody can predict them that closely. The last I heard, the Big One was due sometime in the next fifty years and is more likely to occur in Southern California."

"Good lord, that's a strange football schedule," Jim said.

Sidney suddenly realized what had happened and burst out laughing. "They were talking about two different things. The Big Game, the Berkeley-Stanford one, is next Sunday. The Big One is the next big earthquake. Really big. Like the one we had in 1906."

Jim smiled a bit sheepishly and offered to get Sidney a drink. "How long will it take me to understand this town?" he said as he went off. "Strangest place," Sidney heard him mutter.

Then Jock came by and handed Sidney off to another group. This one contained a partner and his wife who were planning a vacation to South America. They were eager for any suggestions Sidney might have on where to go and what to see. Sidney obliged.

She was just warming up, glowing with enthusiasm, when she caught sight of a familiar dark head from across the room. She finished her sentence and looked up. It was Philip Oliver, and he had evidently just come in, for Jock was talking to him near the door. Sidney's every sense went on alert, tuning in like tiny antennae in his direction. The lawyer's wife was asking, she realized, what kind of clothes she should wear for spring in Rio. Sidney fought down something close to panic and stumbled through an answer. She knew he had not seen her, because she would know it if he had. She would have felt his eyes on her.

She excused herself from the group and made her way to a bedroom, out of sight. Damn, she thought. She'd thought she was ready for anything, resuming her life, picking it up where she had left off, pre–Mr. Chips. But she wasn't ready for this. She had assumed that he had simply returned to his cave or whatever he lived in. He was, after all, the man who never came into the City unless he could help it.

Why hadn't Jock and Dolores told her he would be here? But then, she realized, neither of them knew the reason for her sudden trip to Peru. And she should have figured that Philip would be invited, at least to this party—for hadn't Dolores said it was for partners and clients? At any rate, he'd have no reason to think she'd be there, if he was thinking about her at all, which she doubted.

Seeing her coat lying across the bed, she made a sudden decision. She would flee again. Just for tonight. Not from the rest of her life, just from this chance meeting. Why should she have to suffer through the evening? It would be masochism. She had put in her appearance at the party, just as she had vowed to do as the beginning of her reentry program. And she had satisfied her obligation to Dolores and Jock.

She picked up her coat, walked down the hall, and peeked around the corner into the dining room. The crowd was heavy here, as most of the food was set out on the dining-room table. But she couldn't see Philip Oliver. She knew these condominiums like the palm of her hand. If he was still in the living room, there was only one stretch of archway through which he could see her as she made her way to the kitchen. And in the kitchen was the back door.

Carefully keeping as many people as possible between herself and the crucial arch, she slipped into the kitchen.

Only one of the waiters was there, and he gave her a startled look as she wrenched open the back door and went across the wooden porch and down the long flight of steps. She thought perhaps she heard somebody calling her name. She hoped it wasn't Jock. How embarrassing.

It was foggy, she saw—cold, winter night fog. In the parking lot behind the building, she put on her coat and started for the street. It was oddly deserted, though the hour was relatively early. Even in this residential neighborhood, there were usually people out and about at all hours.

She had parked, by necessity, several blocks away. She was glad to get into the familiar little VW. It started immediately, and the homey sound of its engine, which had always reminded her of a sewing machine, took the loneliness out of the night and made the fog a familiar cocoon.

Strangely, she didn't feel like going home right away. Partly it was because she knew Brice was home. He would hear her coming in and would demand to know why she had left so early. She didn't feel like explaining, at least not right now. And there was something else that kept her from going home, something indefinable that made her feel restless, that made her feel home was not the place to be. She needed to go somewhere and get this out of her system. Almost without thinking about it, she turned the car in the direction of Land's End.

The fog was as thick as she had ever seen it. Cars were moving very slowly, following each other's taillights. Sidney could not see more than fifteen feet in front of her. Occasionally a shape—a tree, a person, the corner of a building—would loom up and as quickly disappear. Traffic lights and street lights and lighted signs glowed only dimly. Sidney inched farther and farther west. The fog didn't bother her, for she knew these streets as well as she knew her own house. At last she saw the light of Cliff House, an indistinct glare in front of her.

It had been her original intention to walk along the wall by Cliff House and see if she could look down on the Seal Rocks, but when she parked her car, it was immediately apparent that she would be able to see nothing. She leaned far over the stone battlement and could hear the waves crashing on the rocks.

It was stupid, it was dangerous, but she decided she had to do it. Everything would be solved if she could just get down to the rock. She'd been to it alone before, and she'd been out on it at night, but never in that combination. She looked down at her thin Italian shoes and realized she'd never make it. Then she remembered the pair of old tennis shoes she kept in the trunk. Along with a yellow slicker. Opening the blunt nose of her car, she dredged out shoes and slicker and did a quick change on the sidewalk. No one was around to stare at her this time. Only crazy people walked down Land's End on nights like this.

She took the easy path down and was immediately certain that there was no one else down there. She could hear the boom of the surf and the regular muffled blast of a foghorn—the one from the lighthouse, for no ship would attempt to sail on a night like this. At the shoreline, the fog was slightly thinner, and there was some faint light coming from Cliff House above. Once she found the narrow causeway, she was home free. She all but ran across it, pulling the slicker tight around her.

She went to the flattest place on the rock and looked down at the water below. She could just make out the iridescent white of the surf. The tide was out, for the water was not very high. She took deep breaths, pulling in the salty tang, the faintly fishy smell.

Sidney sighed. She thought of how the ocean had always fascinated her, had fascinated mankind, perhaps because some scaly ancestor had crawled out of it millions of years before. She thought of how it had always lured people out to adventure, and she wondered if someone, on the other side in far-off Japan, were sitting on a rock, staring at the waves. Suddenly, she didn't feel alone at all.

Then she heard a seal barking, off somewhere in the night. Or thought she did; she could not tell exactly what direction the sound was coming from. It sounded closer the second time than it had the first, so she leaned out and looked down, hoping that the seal was coming to her rock.

She could see no fat flippered form below, so she barked herself. There was no answer. Usually she got one—an answering chorus of sea lions. She was a little disappointed. She was thinking what fun it would be to share a rock in the ocean with a seal when she heard a sound behind her, the sound of a rock scraping another rock. She turned around and saw a human form looming behind her, and then the beam of a flashlight hit her directly in the face, blinding her.

She stood frozen in fear for a second and then took a step backward. Her foot came down on thin air, and she started to go over. She had a split second to hope that she would land in deep water and not on rocks, before a hand shot out and grasped her slicker at the neck. She was yanked painfully back onto her feet and enclosed in strong arms.

"Sidney, it's me. Philip. I didn't mean to frighten you like that. God, I'm sorry." He held her tight. Gradually, she stopped shaking. "Didn't you hear me calling?" he asked.

"I thought you were a seal," she confessed miserably. "I guess that's funny." She braved a smile, but knew he couldn't see it in the fog.

"Not very," he said, holding her even tighter.

Suddenly Sidney was angry. She moved carefully out of his arms. "You nearly got me killed, just now. You scared me half to death."

"And you me," he said. She could just make out that he still had on his dark suit from the party, and a raincoat.

"What are you doing out here?" she snapped.

"Looking for you."

"How did you know I was here?"

"A hunch. I saw you sneak out of the party and figured you'd go home. But when I went there, you hadn't gone there after all. So I came out here and saw your car. And the rest is history."

"Why did you follow me?"

"I want to talk to you."

"And what if I don't want to talk? What if I just want to be out here by myself? This is *my* rock, you know." Sidney could see nothing of his face, only the bulk of him in the swirling fog. "Why don't you just leave me along? Isn't firing me enough? You want more revenge?"

There was a note of surprise in his voice when he said, "But I didn't fire you. You misunderstood. There was simply nothing more for you to do. But I *was* very angry. I apologize for that."

"Then why didn't you tell me so before this?" she snarled, huddling back down on the rock. Now that she had gotten over her fright, she wanted only for him to go away. She would outlast him. She had her slicker over her raincoat and would be warmer. "Go away," she said.

Instead, he sat down beside her. "I tried to tell you, but apparently you had taken off for Peru."

"If you learned that, you could have taken the trouble to locate me. There's the international mail, and there are telephones."

"This needed to be straightened out in person. And I've been busy."

"I can imagine," Sidney said with heavy irony. "Now you can go. You've apologized." She pulled her knees up under the yellow slicker. It was getting cold.

"I'm not leaving without you."

"Oh, yes, you are."

"No," he said. "Whatever else comes of this, I'm not leaving you alone out here. This is sheer stupidity, to be out here at night alone in the fog. You don't know who might be lurking back there in those ruins. And if you fell, nobody would ever know what happened to you. Remember the sign back there."

"I know. 'People have been swept from these rocks and drowned.' Why don't you take a hint?"

"I'll just stay here until you're ready to go." He leaned back.

"It'll be a long wait, in that case," Sidney said, putting her head down on her knees. There was a long silence, broken only by the sound of the water and the muffled foghorns.

She realized she was getting very chilled. She was, in fact, shivering under the slicker. The angle of her head let the damp fog seep down the back of her neck. She shot a glance at Philip. He was sitting, unperturbed, even comfortable. She could just make out his profile. He wasn't shivering at all. He looked as if he were waiting patiently for a plane in the first-class lounge at the airport. Damn him.

"Ready to go?" he asked. She caught the faintest flash of his white teeth. She remembered the first time she'd met him and how she'd hated those perfect teeth, and she recalled the devastating smile. It had hung in her mind like the disembodied grin of the Cheshire cat.

Sidney gave up. She was cold and miserable. And not just from the hard rock and the chilly fog. For she had realized that she wanted him again, and she had to get away from him. And there was no way she could get past him on the rock.

"Okay, I give up. Satisfied?" she snapped, standing up.

He stood, too. "Not yet."

He switched on the flashlight and directed the beam ahead of her onto the causeway. He stayed very close behind her until they reached land, and then he reached out and firmly took her hand.

She tried to shake it off. "I won't fall."

"But I might." And he didn't let go.

When they reached the sidewalk at the top, Sidney tried to pull away again.

"My car is up there," she complained as he pulled her in the opposite direction. They'd been out on the rock longer than she realized, for though the Cliff House lights were still blazing, there were few parked cars.

"Look," she said again, "I just want to go home."

"Not now," he told her. "We're going into Cliff House and get you warmed up. You aren't acting very rationally."

Stung by the obvious truth of that, Sidney went quietly along.

Cliff House was that rare San Francisco phenomenon, a mecca for both tourists and locals. Mark Twain, who was a little of both, had written a long account of the rigors of driving a horse and buggy through miles of blowing sand, where the long, placid, pastel "avenues" now stand, to have breakfast at Cliff House. He found it worth the effort. So had thousands of San Franciscans since.

At night, the ranks of tour buses were gone, the souvenir hawkers who staked out the sidewalks had folded their tables and gone home to the Haight-Ashbury. Inside Cliff House, the lights were dim and rosy over scarred, mismatched old furniture and the long, dark mirrored bar. The walls were covered with autographed pictures of celebrities who had dined there, most of them long-forgotten. Others, like Enrico Caruso and Jenny Lind, recalled the city's Belle Epoque. With its ornate floral carpeting, Tiffany lamps, and drooping Boston ferns, Cliff House had always reminded Sidney of her great aunt Bertha's front parlor. Actually, she didn't have a great aunt Bertha, but if she had, her parlor would have looked like this.

It being a week night, they found a table immediately, a small one, in a corner. It overlooked Ocean Beach, the long, straight stretch of sand whose icy surf and vicious riptides marked the western boundary of the City. Or it would have, had the fog not obscured the view.

"Have you had anything to eat?" Philip asked.

She shook her head. "Not since lunch."

He ordered a plate of cheeses and fruits, and two Irish coffees. He helped her struggle out of her slicker, which had collected and condensed the fog in droplets and was now dripping. Her hair was curling wildly in the damp, and her tennis shoes were a muddy mess. She looked him over covertly. Not one hair of his expensive haircut was out of place, and his suit looked fresh from Brooks Brothers. Even his shoes looked as if he'd just had them shined. His raincoat, which he had dropped across an empty chair, was, of course, a Burberry. She'd always wanted a Burberry raincoat and could never even come close to affording one. Perhaps there *was* something to selling one's soul for money.

Which reminded her. "Shouldn't you be getting back to Silicon Valley?" she said. "It's a week night. You have to get to work in the morning."

"I don't work in Silicon Valley anymore," he replied.

"And I've sublet an apartment in San Francisco for a couple of months."

Sidney was shocked. "You don't *work* there anymore? And you moved to the City? After all you said about it?" Her eyebrows rose.

"It's probably only temporary," he said with a hint of sarcasm.

The waitress set down their drinks and food, and Sidney took a deep sip of her hot, sweet Irish coffee as she tried to digest this new information. Almost instantly she felt the warmth spreading through her body, driving away the chill. Her body temperature and her confidence rose. She took another big swallow.

"You really aren't working at Sunnyvale anymore?" she asked incredulously. "You moved Pacific Instruments?"

"No, I sold my shares. It's not my company anymore."

Sidney took yet another swallow. And took a flying leap to a conclusion. "I'll bet you got a lot richer in the bargain, too, didn't you? Brice told me about the crazy thing your stock did. It's just like you. Did you sell out at the top? When it was over a hundred? Did Max advise you on that, too?"

His green eyes bored into hers. "You really don't like me, do you?"

Sidney picked up a small piece of cheese, chewed on it for a moment, and washed it down with more Irish coffee. What an opportunity he was giving her. Open season on Mr. Chips. Did it ever feel good, Sidney thought.

"Buy me another drink and I'll tell you," she said arrogantly.

"Aren't you downing your first one pretty fast?"

"I'm still cold," she said, "and you nearly got me killed tonight. I think you should buy me another."

He signaled the waitress to bring one more. While he did, she reached over and took his, which was nearly full. She took several deep swallows before handing it back to him. "Now, where were we?" she said.

"I think you were telling me why you don't like me," he said flatly.

"That's right. No, I really don't like you. You're like Max. He'd do anything for money. Before, I thought you might have been trying to prop up your beloved corporation, that that might have driven you. But now I see that even P.I. meant nothing to you. You did some kind of a dirty deal with the South Americans and then sold out."

The drink had appeared at her elbow. She sipped at it, picked up a grape from the plate, and continued. "Furthermore, that's all above and beyond what you did to me. You say you didn't fire me, but it amounted to the same thing." She popped the grape into her mouth.

"Not only that," she said between swallows of grape and coffee, "you think I go around trying to get my name in the papers, calling up Pat Mastodon or whatever her name was. Is. What do you think I am anyway? Your ex-wife? Do you think I went to bed with you to get a piece of Pacific Instruments, like she did?"

She watched carefully as she sipped her drink, waiting to see the effect of that clever thrust, which she considered rapierlike. She would goad him out of that cool facade and into the open.

"It crossed my mind," he said. "But then, you must admit you seem to think I'm exactly like your ex-husband, so I suppose we're even."

Stalemate, Sidney thought. She pondered for a minute and remembered that she had one more shot in her arsenal, one more grievance, that he couldn't top. She swallowed more Irish coffee.

"Also, for your information, you put a big hole in my translation business. I worked excu—excLUsively for you for so long that I lost most of my clients. But I don't suppose I could get a recmend—a reCOmmendation or a referral from you anyway, considering my poor character." She drained the glass.

His hand came across the table and covered hers. She had not expected that, and even as angry as she was, she felt a kind of tingle, a small jolt.

"Sidney, stop it," he said, and there was a warmth in his voice that made her want to dissolve into tears. She looked up, blinking rapidly. He patted her hand in a fatherly manner and told her: "I'll give you all the recommendations you'll ever need. And if I thought you were anything like my ex-wife, I wouldn't be here now."

She looked blurrily across the table at him and saw his solemn, handsome face, with the rakish eyebrows and the chiseled, high-bridged nose and the cleft chin, and then she saw the eyes, the green eyes, and she saw that what was in them was not anger but concern.

"Why did you follow me? It just made everything worse," she said in despair. "I had you out of my system. I don't give a damn about you anymore."

"Does that mean you did give a damn, somewhere along the line?" he asked, looking at her long and hard.

"Yes," she said. "Somewhere along the line I did, I guess. Now I want another drink."

"No, Sidney."

"If you won't buy me one, I'll pay for it myself." She looked around for the waitress.

"Sidney, they're closing up. We have to go."

Then she saw that they were alone in the place and that the bartender had washed all his glasses and put them away. The waitress was turning out the lights one by one and throwing pointed looks in their direction.

He left a big tip on the table, helped her into her slicker, and, taking her arm, walked her outside into the fog. She dimly saw her car sitting all by itself under a street light up the hill. She started toward it.

"No," he said. "I'm taking you home. You've had too much to drink."

"Don't be ridiculous. I can drive," she insisted.

"The last thing you need is a drunk driving citation. You know how tough they are here."

"But I can't leave my car there."

"It'll be fine. You can pick it up in the morning."

When they got into his car, Sidney said, "Heep!"

"Pardon?" he said, looking over at her as he turned the ignition key.

"Nothing," Sidney said.

A moment later, she said "Heep!" again.

He threw her a puzzled look.

"I've got the hiccups," she said. "Heep!"

"For God's sake, I never heard anyone hiccup like that before!"

She looked at him imperiously. "I am polylingual. I hiccup in Spanish."

Then she looked straight ahead, in order to ignore his valiant efforts to keep a straight face as he drove her to her house. She heeped most of the way.

He walked her to her door and helped her unlock it.

"Will you be okay?" he asked.

"I'll be fine, thanks," she said.

"I probably won't see you again," he said. "I'm going to move back to New York."

"Good," she said. "That's where you belong."

CHAPTER FIFTEEN

SIDNEY SLEPT VERY late the next morning and woke with a headache. She resisted the temptation to drink a Coke for breakfast, telling herself she did not, repeat *did not*, have a hangover. Bacon and eggs and two aspirin washed down with several cups of black coffee and a large glass of orange juice helped considerably.

She sat at the kitchen table in her faded Levi's and an old T-shirt that said DISREGARD PREVIOUS T-SHIRTS and made a neat list of things to do and people to call in order to get her business under way again. She was chewing thoughtfully on her pencil when the phone rang.

"This is Jim, from the Eddys' party," said a pleasant voice from the other end of the line. "I went looking for a drink for you, and you disappeared."

Sidney felt slightly guilty. "Oh," she said. "I, uh, wasn't feeling well and decided to slip out. I'm sorry. I couldn't find you in the crowd to tell you." It wasn't quite a lie, she thought. She *had* thought about finding him, for a fleeting moment.

"I hope you're okay now." he said.

"Oh, yes," she answered. "I'm fine now.

"Say, listen. I got your number from Dolores, and I was wondering if you'd like to go sailing with me Saturday, provided the weather forecast is right."

Sidney wasn't sure she wanted to go anywhere with anyone at that moment. "I'm not very good at sailing," she temporized. "I get tangled up in all those ropes."

"Sheets," Jim corrected. "Sheets are what you get tangled up in."

"I beg your pardon?" Sidney said.

"Ropes on a boat are called sheets, and halyards. I can tell you haven't sailed much." He laughed. "But I'd be happy to teach you how."

Sidney thought a minute. He wasn't devastatingly handsome, but he was passable. He wasn't dashing and overwhelmingly sexy, but he was nice. And he wasn't from New York.

"In that case," she said, "I'd love to."

"Great," he said enthusiastically. "Do you happen to own any foul-weather gear? You'll need it, this time of year."

"I only have a slicker," she replied, and blurry memories of the night before came pushing at the edges of her mind. In her efforts to suppress them, she didn't hear all of what he said thereafter. It was something about his having some gear in her size. He would be in touch later that week.

At least, she thought, hanging up the phone, that was something to look forward to. She'd been sailing a few times and had liked it. She was surefooted on deck. She didn't get seasick. She'd always said she wanted to learn how to sail. Maybe it was a good omen. Then again, maybe it wasn't. It could be said, she thought, that getting tangled in the sheets had been her downfall with Philip Oliver.

But meanwhile, there was the little matter of making a living. She called the medical school and told them she was back in town, and they said they would pass the word around and she'd have something in a few days. More gall bladders, probably, she thought. Or maybe she'd be lucky and get a report on the pancreas or on some interesting, gruesome tropical disease. She liked variety in her work.

She made several more phone calls, but nobody seemed to be in. She paced around the kitchen and then, on an impulse, opened the refrigerator, which brought both cats running. "Refrigerator worshipers," she said, pushing them away. She found what she was looking for: a large sirloin steak. She took it out of the freezer compartment and called Brice at work.

"Hey," she said. "I want to invite you to dinner tonight."

He sounded slightly surprised. "What brought this on? You never invite me over for dinner."

"I know," she told him. "You just eat here without being invited. This time I'm doing a dinner planned just for you. I'm thinking of making an apple pie, even. And my motive is guilt."

"Guilt?" Brice asked, amazement in his voice.

"Yep. Guilt. I never thanked you for taking care of my house when I was gone. Not that you did much of a job."

"That's very gracious of you, Sidney," he said. "Is there anything you want me to bring?"

"Just your gorgeous little old self," she replied.

He grunted. "Okay, count me in."

She spent the rest of the afternoon making an apple pie from scratch. For some reason she'd always associated steak and mashed potatoes and apple pie with Peoria. She felt that she wanted to do something really nice for Brice, and this would remind him of his hometown.

She told him that when he came sauntering in. He raised his black eyebrows and said, "Things have changed in Peoria. And my mother didn't make apple pie, if that's what you're thinking. She's a crackerjack cordon bleu cook. You know, duck à l'orange, that kind of thing."

But he liked the steak and potatoes and apple pie anyway, he said afterward. And it had been a nice gesture. They lingered over coffee, and Brice said, "By the way, you might be interested in this. Rumor has it that your ex, Max, took a bath in Pacific Instruments stock."

Sidney sat up straight. "Is that right? How did that happen?"

Brice grinned. "Well, you know the secret of making money on the stock market. Very simple. Buy low and sell high. I guess he did the opposite."

"Tell me more!"

"Well, it's all rumor, of course, and I really don't know much. But P.I. stock was so volatile that first day that my guess is he got his order in late, bought on margin, forgot to put in a stop loss order. Or maybe the wire was too full to get the order in before profit takers knocked the price down, and he got a big margin call."

"So he lost his shirt, and owes his undershirt to the brokerage house. Poor Max."

"Well, somewhat poorer, anyway," Brice said.

"Brice." Sidney was thoughtful. "Have you heard any rumors about Mr. Chips? You know he sold his shares."

Brice nodded.

"Did he unload it at the top of the market? At a hundred and five or whatever it went to?"

"No, that's the funny thing. He sold his shares back to the corporation before the stock went on the market. It was a private transaction. He probably got less than ten dollars a share for it. The odd thing is that he had to have known that stock was going to go hog wild—that new laser process really is a breakthrough, they say. Apparently he didn't want to be rich and famous."

"Or rich and infamous," Sidney said, but she was thinking hard. "Do you happen to know if the deal went through in South America? Did they open an assembly plant down there?"

Brice said, puzzled, "I figured that was what you were doing up at Timber Cove. Working on something like that. You mean you don't know?"

"I was, uh, laid off, right in the middle of the discussions," she said.

"So that's it." Brice looked at her speculatively. "Well, the answer to that is, I don't know. But I doubt it. From what I understand about the new process, it's capital-intensive, not labor-intensive. That means..."

"You don't have to explain everything," Sidney said in

annoyance. "That means that if they have the new process to make computer chips here in the U.S., then they don't need the plant in South America."

Brice nodded. "And they got the capital for the new equipment from the stock issue."

But Sidney wasn't listening. She was staring at the floor, as if the pattern of the Persian rug contained the secret of the universe. So he hadn't gotten rich from his Pacific Instruments stock. And he hadn't done a deal with the sleazy South Americans, and he hadn't been in cahoots with Max. She'd figured it all wrong. Still, there was the ugly scene in his suite at Timber Cove, where he'd all but accused her of . . . what had he accused her of, exactly? Then she heard Brice saying, "Earth to Sidney, Earth to Sidney. Come in."

"What?" she said, looking up.

"Hey, space cadet. What are you thinking about so hard?"

Sidney sighed. "I'm thinking I owe Philip Oliver an apology."

"You've seen him, then?"

"Yes, last night. He was at the party," she fudged.

"What happened?"

"I called him all kinds of bad names, most of which he didn't deserve."

"Well, why don't you just apologize?"

"I can't. I don't know how to reach him, and he's leaving for New York, and I'm too damn proud. Anyway, I never want to lay eyes on him again."

"Sidney, listen to me," Brice said, his tone stern and serious. "Apologize to him. You'll never forgive yourself if you don't."

She looked at him suspiciously. "Do you know something I don't?"

"Yes," he said, but he wouldn't say any more.

And so it was that Sidney was once again preparing to ride the bus on her way to see Philip Oliver. She'd gotten his phone number and address from Dolores, who had not seemed surprised. "He found you, then?" was all Dolores said, and Sidney didn't have time to worry about the implications of the remark. She'd called the number twice, and both times it was busy, which, Brice pointed out, suggested he was home.

So she'd decided to go and see him. At once. Before she lost her courage, before she could think about it.

She grabbed her purse from the kitchen table and an old parka from the coat rack, and ran out the front door. She stood at the curb for half a minute, peering up and down the street, trying to remember where she'd parked and wondering if her car had been stolen. Only then did she remember that it was still in front of Cliff House, two miles away. Without stopping to worry about it, she ran down the hill to the bus stop. As she arrived, breathless, the Number 23 was just pulling away from the curb. She pounded frantically on the doors, and to her astonishment, the driver stopped and let her on. She didn't like to ride the Muni at night, alone. But this was a safe route, and Philip Oliver's address belonged to a good neighborhood, so she risked it.

The address Dolores had given her turned out to be a new apartment building wedged between old mansions, some converted to private schools. It sat on top of the hills that were always referred to in the guidebooks as "exclusive Pacific Heights." The view must be terrific, Sidney thought as she looked up at the building. She went into the entryway and studied the names on the mailboxes. She saw no "Oliver," but remembered Philip mentioning he'd sublet the apartment. He'd probably forgotten to change the name. She checked the slip again and saw Dolores had given her the apartment number. She pressed the button marked 501 on the panel beside the door.

After a while, there was a scratching sound from the intercom speaker embedded in the wall, and Philip's voice said, "Yes?"

"It's me, Sidney. Can I come in?" she said to the wall.

There was no answer from the intercom, but the door buzzed open, and she grabbed it quickly and went in. She decided to take the stairs instead of the elevator, to work off some of the dinner, and as she reached the top, panting a little, she found him waiting for her outside his door. He, too, was dressed in jeans and a faded gray sweat shirt that had stamped across it in bold letters: "NOT TO BE TAKEN FROM THE GYM, PROPERTY OF M.I.T." He looked tired, and his hair was mussed, as if he or someone else, had been running a hand through it. He was smiling very faintly.

Suddenly Sidney's heart was in her shoes. She shouldn't have come here. What was the matter with her? He probably had a woman inside, she thought. He wouldn't let her in.

But he said, "Come on in," so she did. She stopped dead in the doorway, struck with something akin to awe when she saw the interior. It was not an apartment, she thought, it was an adult playground. White shag carpeting lay inches deep on the floor, enormous overstuffed twin sofas flanked a fireplace with a real bear rug in front of it, and one entire wall was made up of a wet bar, an oversized TV screen, an elaborate sound system, and hundreds of Betamax tapes, filed under "X", "XX," and "XXX."

"That's called an entertainment wall," he said, evidently noticing that she was studying it in astonishment. "Come and see the rest. It'll knock you dead."

The bedroom contained an enormous waterbed, a remote-control TV angled above it, and another bar, but it was the bathroom that rocked her the most. Along with the usual equipment, it contained a Jacuzzi big enough for four. This fixture, and all the others, had elaborate gold handles shaped like nude women. The wallpaper showed friezes of couples in various, and astonishing, sexual positions.

"That's an exact reproduction of the famous murals at Pompeii," Philip explained as Sidney gaped. "Take a good look. At Pompeii they won't let women in to see them."

Sidney looked at him suspiciously. "Did it look like this when you moved in?" she asked.

He laughed. "I'm afraid it did. I didn't have much choice. There aren't too many people who are willing to sublet a furnished apartment for less than a year at a time."

"But who is he? Your landlord, I mean?" she persisted.

"I've never even seen him. I rented it though an agency. I think he's a lawyer for a rock group, and he's with them on a European tour. Wouldn't you like to meet him?"

"No," Sidney said with conviction.

"Why don't you come into the kitchen?" Philip said, moving away. "I seem to be spending most of my time there. Do you want a drink?"

Sidney flinched.

"How about some coffee, then?"

"Coffee's fine," she said, following him down the hall to the kitchen. At least a kitchen was impossible to turn into a sexual playroom, she was thinking. She looked around and saw that it was conventional, almost bare. There was nothing on the counter but the remains of a TV dinner. The dishwasher door was open, and Sidney could see three or four glasses inside.

"My landlord didn't have any dishes or silverware. I bought a frying pan and a coffeepot." He showed her a totally empty cupboard. "I eat out a lot."

"What a lifestyle," Sidney said. Then she saw that the kitchen table had been pushed over against the wall, under the telephone, and that it held a portable computer terminal. The screen flickered. She walked over, half-expecting to see Pac-Man. But the screen contained long rows of white capital letters following numbered lines. And the phone receiver was cradled in a plastic hollow in the side of the terminal. Which accounted for the line being busy, Sidney thought. There was a stack of blank computer printout paper on the table, covered with penciled writing. So that was what he'd been doing when she'd interrupted him, she thought.

"What's this?" she said.

"That's called a CRT," he said from beside the stove, where he was heating the coffee.

"I know it's a CRT," she said. "What are you programming on it?"

"Nothing much," he said offhandedly. "Just trying out an idea I had for a 256K chip."

"That's the next big jump, isn't it?" she asked.

He swung around, looking at her in surprise. "You know about that?"

"Not a whole lot," Sidney told him. "But I do know that a chip is a computer memory, and that a bit is a piece of information on a chip, and that so far, they've only been able to get sixty-four thousand bits on a chip. When they get the 256-thousand bit chip, NASA will be able to do moon launches from a hand-held computer."

He looked at her, clearly impressed. "Not quite. But close." Then his voice dropped. "You never cease to amaze me."

He poured the coffee, handed her a cup, and switched off the CRT. "When I sold out of P.I., I made a deal whereby I could still plug into their mainframe computer. I'd be lost without it."

He tilted his head. "Let's sit in the living room. I don't think I've ever been in it yet."

Sidney sat down on one couch, and he sat on the other. Between them was a vast glass coffee table. Slick, expensive-looking art books were laid out on it. The title of the one closest to Sidney was *Erotic Art of the Ming Dynasty*. She peered at the four-color picture beautifully reproduced on its dust jacket. She was wondering what on earth the man in the picture was doing with his big toe, when Philip said, "Tell me, now that you've had the tour, to what do I owe the honor of this visit?"

Sidney took a deep breath. "I came to apologize," she said.

"Oh?" He was sipping his coffee and looking at her blandly over the rim of his cup.

"I was wrong about you. I called you all kinds of names. And I want to apologize. I found out you sold your stock before it ever went on the market. And some other things." She couldn't look at him.

"How did you hear that?" he asked.

"Brice told me. He must have gotten it from that rumor mill down on Montgomery Street, the one you're so crazy about."

"No, he probably read that one in the *Wall Street Journal*," Philip said. "That was legitimate news."

"There's something else I think I have to apologize for," she sighed. "But I need some information first."

"You mean you wouldn't want to apologize for anything

you didn't have to?" His voice was flat.

"No. Well, yes," Sidney said. This wasn't going the way she'd expected it to. There was a failure of communication. She knew seven languages, and she couldn't seem to get anything across to him.

"Did you carry through on the South American deal?" she asked.

"No. I broke it off right after you left. Well, actually before you left Timber Cove."

"But why didn't you tell me that?" she asked, almost plaintively.

"I didn't want you involved. You were supposed to be the interpreter, and you had no business getting involved. I had pretty much decided the night before that I was going to break off the negotiations, but I wanted to see what Guillame had to say about the details of the financing. I couldn't believe my ears." He looked at her grimly. "Saving the corporation never came before my own principles, despite what you may think. Max and I had been discussing— more like arguing—something like that when you came crashing in."

"I didn't crash in. I still want to know why you didn't tell me you were breaking them off at the time."

"Mostly because we hadn't told the South Americans yet, and it seemed to me to be a matter of courtesy, at least, to tell them first."

"I see that," said Sidney. "I guess that makes sense."

"I think it does. Or did at the time." He was looking at her expectantly.

"So they all left shortly after I did?" Sidney was thinking.

"Right on your heels. Max and Alicia stayed on for a few days in San Francisco, I think."

"And what did you do?" Sidney persisted.

"Me? I went to Sunnyvale to set up another strategic plan. Or would that be a tactical plan? You tell me—you're the one who's getting an M.B.A."

"I haven't had that course yet," she snapped, stung at the tone of his voice.

"So now I get another apology, right?"

Sidney was feeling worse and worse, if possible. The conversation had gotten completely out of her control, and he was angry. Maybe he had a right to be, but so did she.

She said, "Right," and stood up and headed for the kitchen. "Now that *that's* over, I'm going home." She reached for the telephone. "How do you disconnect this thing?" she asked, realizing it was still hooked up to the computer.

"Who do you want to call?" he asked.

"A taxi," she said. "I've got to get home and do the dishes."

He'd followed her into the kitchen and looked at her sharply. "You want to call a cab? Where's your car?"

"Still at Cliff House," she admitted gloomily. "I forgot about it."

"How did you get here?" he asked.

"On the Muni. The Twenty-three Haight, to be exact."

He laughed, but it was a little harsh, Sidney thought.

"Sidney, sometimes I think you need a keeper." He picked up her parka from the kitchen chair where she had left it, and held it out. "Come on, I'll take you to your car."

"If it's still there," she said.

It wasn't. He drove slowly past the line of cars parked at the curb by Cliff House. None of them was hers.

Sidney pointed at an empty space. "It was right there. Oh, lord, what do I do now?" She groaned.

Philip pulled into the parking place. "It's probably been towed. And in that case, you'd probably call the police garage."

"I suppose you're right. Nobody would steal that clunker," she said despondently.

"Do you want to go into Cliff House and have a drink? That might cheer you up. And you could use their phone," he pointed out.

"No," she said. "That's the last thing I want to do. And anyway, the police garage is closed this time of night."

She looked out at the empty sidewalk. There was no fog tonight, and she could see the stars over the Marin headlands. But even the stars looked bleak and miserable to Sidney. She was on the verge of tears. How *could* she have been so stupid?

"I had three parking tickets already. I'll bet there are ten more, plus the towing charge. They'll probably throw me in jail," she moaned. "I can't afford fines like that."

"Poor Sidney," Philip said. "We'll get your car back, don't worry." He put an arm around her shoulder and patted her as he would a small child. She moved a bit in his direction and found herself with her head on his shoulder.

"I know how you feel," he said. "I've been miserable, too. Ever since you walked out that door at Timber Cove, in fact."

"At least you still have a car," Sidney wailed, and then she stopped. "What did you say?"

"I said I've been miserable ever since you left Timber Cove."

"Me, too," Sidney said. She looked up and saw him break into his fabulous lopsided grin, and saw the wild surmise in his eyes. The horrid leaden lump that had been sitting for weeks where her heart had once been now melted, along with any thought that she did not love this man.

He kissed her long and hard, and then looked down at her. He shook his handsome head and said, "What fools we mortals be!"

He stroked her hair and kissed her on each eye, on her forehead, her nose, and her neck. He leaned back, and she found herself lying against him, the steering wheel pushing into her back.

"I'm glad you don't have bucket seats." She giggled and pulled his head down and kissed him back. He slid his hand under her parka and T-shirt and unhooked her brassiere, and she was tensing in delicious anticipation of the feel of his hand on her breast when there was a bang on the top of the car. Through the window a light shone directly on her face.

"Cheese it, the cops," Philip said. Quickly, Sidney buried her face in his windbreaker. He rolled down the window and asked, "What can I do for you, Officer?"

"You can move along," said a rough voice. "Scram. I have enough trouble with teenagers along here as it is. You guys are too old for this."

"It's okay, Officer," Philip said, and Sidney could hear amusement in his voice. "We're getting married."

"That don't make no difference to me. Just go park in somebody else's district. Go to a hotel. You look like you can afford it." The cop turned out the flashlight and walked away, handcuffs clinking.

Sidney sat up as well as she could and looked at Philip in astonishment. "Why did you tell him we were getting married?"

"Because it seemed like a good idea at the time. How about it?"

"How about what?" Sidney croaked.

"Do you think it's a good idea? Or to put it another way, will you marry me?"

Sidney thought about it for a long time, perhaps ten seconds.

"Yes," she said.

He reached for her and kissed her, a joyous, glorious, all-encompassing, possessive kiss to end all kisses. Suddenly a blinding glare came through the back window of the car. Sidney shaded her eyes and squinted into it. "He's got the spotlight from his squad car on us," she said.

"I guess he means it," Philip said, letting go of Sidney and starting the car. "Where to now? My place or yours?"

Sidney didn't hesitate a second. "Yours. It's perfect for what I've got in mind."

"Then," he said, putting the car in reverse, "in the immortal words of Noel Coward, let's do it!"

"It was Cole Porter," said Sidney.

CHAPTER SIXTEEN

THEY TRIED THE waterbed first and found it highly satisfactory. Then they studied the Pompeiian wallpaper. "Your average Roman must have been in better shape then we are," Philip said. They tried the Jacuzzi, and eventually agreed that the idea was wonderful in the abstract but somewhat dangerous and uncomfortable in the reality.

"Your tan is fading," Sidney said as he toweled himself off. "Or your teeth are getting tarnished."

"There's no tennis court here. Also, no sun. I'll have to join a health club or something. I need the exercise." He was now drying her, tenderly, handling her as if she were made of fine porcelain.

"I've got a better idea for exercise," she said, pulling on the towel. "This way." She dragged him down the hall as he clutched the towel.

When the waterbed stopped swaying and sloshing and Sidney had sunk through clouds of rapture into something more like everyday crazy-in-love insane happiness, she lay next to him with her head on his shoulder and asked, as lovers always will, "Who were you going out with the night I met you?"

"Hmmm?" he said distantly. He was lazily stroking her. "Your skin is like silk. Amazing."

"Philip, who stood you up at Ernie's that night? Was it a *princesa*?"

He kissed her. "Jealous, are you? Well, don't be. It was my former wife. She wanted to meet me in town about something. I guess it was to tell me she got her steamship heir."

"You never talk about her, do you?" Sidney ventured.

"There isn't much to say," he said. "She wanted money and social position, and she got it. I wish her well, I guess. It's hard to talk about it, still."

"I know," Sidney said, hugging him.

"I think a lot of it was my fault. She wasn't that way when I met her. She was fresh and bright, right out of college. I hired her. The corporation was just starting to take off, and it was exciting, seeing how far you could take it. The sky was the limit. Then it wasn't so much fun anymore. We'd made it, that was the trouble. I turned into a manager and had to work terrible hours, doing things I didn't particularly like to do. She got bored, and I wasn't paying that much attention to her. She began to play corporation president's wife, and liked it. I didn't want to go into the City every night or try to get into the Burlingame Country Club or the Olympic. Or be seen at Ernie's." There was a faint bitterness in his voice, and he had pulled away from her a little.

"You thought I was like that?" Sidney asked. "You must have thought so when all that stuff came out in the papers. You thought I was trying to get money and social position through you."

"Well," he said, holding her close again and laughing, "the joke's on you. I don't have any social position, and not all that much money." He kissed her. "I knew you didn't plant those articles. I knew that San Francisco is the only city of seven hundred thousand people who all know each other. The best way to make the newspapers here is to try to stay out of them."

"So why did you insinuate I'd planted them?" Sidney was the one who pulled back now.

"I was mad at you," he said. "And I'm willing to spend the rest of my days making it up to you for what I said. Come back here."

"Not until you tell me why you were mad," Sidney said. "I think we're having a fight."

"No, listen to me." He pulled her back to him and held her so tightly she could barely breathe. "At Timber Cove, your husband—your ex, I mean—kept dropping so many insinuations about you that I couldn't help noticing how decent you were being about him. I didn't like him for that. He set my teeth on edge, frankly, even when I saw him in New York. On his own turf. But he's considered one of the best at what he does. The New York Consulting Group is highly respected. But the more he said about you, the more I disliked him, and the more Guillame said about Piedras Negras, the more I disliked *him*. What a crew that was: Max, His Excellency, the fiery Eva, the lovely Alicia, and the Marx Brothers."

Sidney giggled. "I thought they were the three blind mice."

"After we are married," he said into her hair, "I will not allow you to make better jokes than I do. Not that that was all that good." He kissed her lightly and then more deeply. "But to get back to the matter at hand. You came walking in and acted as if I either had been taken in by the wily Max or was just like him. I was either stupid or unprincipled. Your lack of faith was shattering. I thought you loved me, from the way you acted."

"Oh, but I did," Sidney whispered. "And I do."

"I know," he said. "I know now."

There was a silence, interspersed with a few monosyllables, and Philip said, "Do you want to try the bear rug?"

In the warm comfortable exhaustion that followed, Sidney asked, as lovers will, "When did you first decide you wanted to marry me?"

"The fourth time I saw you," he answered instantly. "I've thought about it. You were standing on top of that cliff, above the Sutro Baths, dusting your hands off. The wind was in your hair, and you were watching me."

"That was the fifth time."

"It was the fourth, if you count the first day we met as one event."

"Okay, so why did you want to marry me then?"

"Because you looked so brave, proud, funny, and scared."

"Scared? Me?"

"Yes, you." He put a finger under her chin and tilted her head up and kissed her soundly. "I wanted to put my arms around you and hold you and tell you that I could make it all go away. That I'd take care of you forever."

"Why didn't you, then?"

"Because you are such a knot-headed, sharp-tongued, mixed-up, accident-prone—" He stopped, obviously searching for a word.

"Klutz?" she supplied.

"Yes, klutz."

"Sing me more songs," she said, snuggling into his shoulder and stretching out as far as she could to feel the full, lean length of him. "Tell me more."

"Well," he said, "I didn't dare tell you I wanted to marry you. You were so scared of commitments, remember? Telling me you nearly went into shock on your wedding day was pretty convincing."

"It was your commitment, not mine, that worried me. I didn't think you cared."

"I wasn't sure how *you* felt until we got to Timber Cove."

"Did you arrange all that on purpose?" Sidney asked. "I mean, hire me with that in mind?"

"If I were that good a forecaster, I'd make millions. Nope. I'm not really a manipulator anyway. I did sort of hope that working together would make you somewhat less afraid of me."

Sidney sighed and stirred in his arms. "And then you threw me out at Timber Cove."

"I regretted it the minute I did it. I planned to get hold of you as soon as I had packed them all off, and then I found you had gone to Peru, and I knew I'd blown it."

"Why didn't you call?"

"Dolores advised against it. She said you'd need to work it out and that I should wait until you got back."

"Dolores!" Sidney gasped. "You talked to Dolores."

"Yes," he said. "I even talked to Brice."

"What is this, a conspiracy?" Sidney said, aghast. "When did you talk to Brice?"

"When I went over to anchor your grandfather clock. You noticed, didn't you?" Sidney shook her head. Observant, wasn't she? But she hadn't.

"It was driving me crazy, thinking about it sitting there," he continued.

"Brice let me in, and watched to make sure I didn't steal anything, and we talked. He's a nice guy. He approves of our marriage."

"You mean I was the last to know?"

"Yes." Philip smiled.

Sidney lay back and contemplated the plaster on the ceiling, then sat up hurriedly and said, "You really fixed my grandfather clock?"

"Yes. I've always been good with my hands." And then he showed her that he was.

In the morning, he put on a bathrobe and loaned her one of his T-shirts, which reached nearly to her knees. They went into the kitchen and tried to figure out how to have breakfast when there weren't any dishes.

"I suppose we could call out for Chinese," Sidney suggested.

"Ugh," Philip said.

They settled on coffee, toast, and fried eggs eaten directly from the pan. They sat on the bear rug in the living room, sharing the single fork. It was a beautiful, golden day, and when Philip drew the drapes, they could see the entire bay from the Golden Gate Bridge to Treasure Island. A few sailboats were venturing out into a stiff breeze.

Suddenly, Sidney remembered something. "We'll have to postpone our wedding."

"Why's that?" Philip asked with some concern.

"I promised I'd go sailing Saturday."

"That's okay." he said. "City Hall isn't open Saturday anyway. That's where we'll get married, of course. But there's a three-day waiting period, too. We'll have to wait till Monday."

"You've got it all figured out, do you?" Sidney laughed.

"Yep. Unless you want to go to Reno, but I thought you'd want to get married in your beloved City."

"Oh!" Sidney cried in horror. "I just remembered something else! You're moving back to New York, aren't you? Well, I won't leave here. Not even for you."

"I figured you could commute on weekends." He grinned. "You could take the red-eye special every Friday. Airline pilots do it all the time."

"I sincerely hope you're kidding," Sidney said, suddenly nervous.

He leaned over the coffee cups and the frying pan to kiss her on the nose. "Of course I am. I was planning to move back there if you didn't relent and marry me, but I got to thinking about it even before that. I think I've caught the California Disease. I have filed my application papers for San Francisco citizenship."

"But I thought you sold your corporation because you wanted to move back East!" Sidney exclaimed in surprise.

"No, I sold it because I realized I didn't like being a captain of industry. I want to go back to being a civilian. I also want more time to spend doing the things I like to do and I wanted to get back to my first love." He paused and then smiled at the look on her face. "No, not *her*. R and D. Research and development. As soon as we nailed down that laser process and I knew the corporation was going to stay afloat, I got out. Not completely; I'm still on the roster as a consultant. But I can consult anywhere. As long as I can find a telephone to plug that thing into." He nodded toward the CRT.

Sidney grinned. "Well, that takes care of you. But how about me? I want to finish school and become a big-time hotshot international consultant."

"Sure, go ahead. You get the jet lag, I'll keep the home fires burning."

Sidney dabbed up the last bit of egg yolk with the last piece of toast. "By the way," she said sweetly. "Do you know what the qualifications for San Francisco citizenship are?"

"I've been studying the manual."

"And?" she challenged.

"Let's see," he said thoughtfully, draining his coffee mug. "Never do any work on Monday morning or Friday afternoon, complain about the Muni, always walk against the light, celebrate every imaginable holiday in the streets, and say 'Only in San Francisco' whenever anything happens. How'm I doing?"

"So far, so good," she said. "But you forgot that you have to run in the Bay to Breakers marathon dressed as a box of Velveeta—"

"Or the flying nun," he interrupted.

"And take visitors down the Fillmore Street hill in your car."

"To hear them scream in terror," he added.

"And you have to pretend that you don't like 'I Left My Heart in San Francisco.'"

"And don't forget," he said, "that you have to be on a first-name basis with your plumber and your senator and all your neighbors, and you have to go down to complain at Park and Bark—"

Sidney said, "It's Park and Rec. The Commission on Parks and Recreation. There's also the Board of Supervisors, the Planning Commission, the Board of Permit Appeals, the Arts Commission—"

"Enough!" he interjected. "I know I'll have to do a lot of complaining here. And I'll also have to buy bad wine from Boston, instead of the Napa Valley, live in a mud hut with a dirt floor, wear pantaloons, and do fandangos." He sobered for a moment and looked at her very seriously.

"And raise our kids to be Californians?" he asked.

She thought about it for a minute and said, "Is there any other way?"

He smiled at her for a long moment. "They're doomed anyway, he said at last. "They'll be fourth-generation lazy on your side."

"Lucky little devils." Sidney smiled.

He reached out to touch her face and looked at her with so much love in his eyes that she thought she'd drown in them. Then, with obvious effort, he dropped his hand and said, "Let's clean up." He picked up the frying pan.

"Fine, but after that I have to go home and do my own dishes and feed the cats and call about my car."

He stood up. "And what do you plan to do after that?"

"Get married, I guess. On Monday."

"In that case, I guess I'd better go with you. And make sure you show up."

While Sidney was scraping the frying pan into the garbage disposal, she felt a faint wave of dizziness sweep over her. She put the pan in the sink and walked to the doorway of the kitchen, where Philip was already standing, looking thoughtful.

As the building began to sway in earnest, he said, "Five will get you ten that this one is less than four-point-five on the Richter scale."

Sidney looked up at him and grinned. "You just passed your final for citizenship."

"How's that?" he said.

"You just did what San Franciscans do about earthquakes."

"And what's that?"

"We bet on them."

He grinned his glorious grin and held her tight and said, "There's really not much else you can do about them, is there?" Then his face changed, and he became very solemn. He fixed her with a falcon stare, cocking an eyebrow, and said, "By the way, there's something I've never told you about me."

"What's that?" Sidney said in alarm.

"I love you," he said. He bent his dark, elegant head and kissed her while the coffee cups danced on the counter and the windows shivered and the sailboats on the bay tacked into the wind, unaware that anything earthshaking was going on in the City.

Second Chance at Love

___ 06540-4 FROM THE TORRID PAST #49 Ann Cristy
___ 06544-7 RECKLESS LONGING #50 Daisy Logan
___ 05851-3 LOVE'S MASQUERADE #51 Lillian Marsh
___ 06148-4 THE STEELE HEART #52 Jocelyn Day
___ 06422-X UNTAMED DESIRE #53 Beth Brookes
___ 06651-6 VENUS RISING #54 Michelle Roland
___ 06595-1 SWEET VICTORY #55 Jena Hunt
___ 06575-7 TOO NEAR THE SUN #56 Aimée Duvall
___ 05625-1 MOURNING BRIDE #57 Lucia Curzon
___ 06411-4 THE GOLDEN TOUCH #58 Robin James
___ 06596-X EMBRACED BY DESTINY #59 Simone Hadary
___ 06660-5 TORN ASUNDER #60 Ann Cristy
___ 06573-0 MIRAGE #61 Margie Michaels
___ 06650-8 ON WINGS OF MAGIC #62 Susanna Collins
___ 05816-5 DOUBLE DECEPTION #63 Amanda Troy
___ 06675-3 APOLLO'S DREAM #64 Claire Evans
___ 06689-3 SWEETER THAN WINE #78 Jena Hunt
___ 06690-7 SAVAGE EDEN #79 Diane Crawford
___ 06692-3 THE WAYWARD WIDOW #81 Anne Mayfield
___ 06693-1 TARNISHED RAINBOW #82 Jocelyn Day
___ 06694-X STARLIT SEDUCTION #83 Anne Reed
___ 06695-8 LOVER IN BLUE #84 Aimée Duvall
___ 06696-6 THE FAMILIAR TOUCH #85 Lynn Lawrence
___ 06697-4 TWILIGHT EMBRACE #86 Jennifer Rose
___ 06698-2 QUEEN OF HEARTS #87 Lucia Curzon
___ 06851-9 A MAN'S PERSUASION #89 Katherine Granger
___ 06852-7 FORBIDDEN RAPTURE #90 Kate Nevins
___ 06853-5 THIS WILD HEART #91 Margarett McKean
___ 06854-3 SPLENDID SAVAGE #92 Zandra Colt
___ 06855-1 THE EARL'S FANCY #93 Charlotte Hines
___ 06858-6 BREATHLESS DAWN #94 Susanna Collins
___ 06859-4 SWEET SURRENDER #95 Diana Mars
___ 06860-8 GUARDED MOMENTS #96 Lynn Fairfax
___ 06861-6 ECSTASY RECLAIMED #97 Brandy LaRue
___ 06862-4 THE WIND'S EMBRACE #98 Melinda Harris
___ 06863-2 THE FORGOTTEN BRIDE #99 Lillian Marsh
___ 06864-0 A PROMISE TO CHERISH #100 LaVyrle Spencer
___ 06866-7 BELOVED STRANGER #102 Michelle Roland
___ 06867-5 ENTHRALLED #103 Ann Cristy
___ 06869-1 DEFIANT MISTRESS #105 Anne Devon
___ 06870-5 RELENTLESS DESIRE #106 Sandra Brown
___ 06871-3 SCENES FROM THE HEART #107 Marie Charles

SK 41 a

_____ 06872-1 **SPRING FEVER #108** Simone Hadary
_____ 06873-X **IN THE ARMS OF A STRANGER #109** Deborah Joyce
_____ 06874-8 **TAKEN BY STORM #110** Kay Robbins
_____ 06899-3 **THE ARDENT PROTECTOR #111** Amanda Kent
_____ 07200-1 **A LASTING TREASURE #112** Cally Hughes $1.95
_____ 07203-6 **COME WINTER'S END #115** Claire Evans $1.95
_____ 07212-5 **SONG FOR A LIFETIME #124** Mary Haskell $1.95
_____ 07213-3 **HIDDEN DREAMS #125** Johanna Phillips $1.95
_____ 07214-1 **LONGING UNVEILED #126** Meredith Kingston $1.95
_____ 07215-X **JADE TIDE #127** Jena Hunt $1.95
_____ 07216-8 **THE MARRYING KIND #128** Jocelyn Day $1.95
_____ 07217-6 **CONQUERING EMBRACE #129** Ariel Tierney $1.95
_____ 07218-4 **ELUSIVE DAWN #130** Kay Robbins $1.95
_____ 07219-2 **ON WINGS OF PASSION #131** Beth Brookes $1.95
_____ 07220-6 **WITH NO REGRETS #132** Nuria Wood $1.95
_____ 07221-4 **CHERISHED MOMENTS #133** Sarah Ashley $1.95
_____ 07222-2 **PARISIAN NIGHTS #134** Susanna Collins $1.95
_____ 07233-0 **GOLDEN ILLUSIONS #135** Sarah Crewe $1.95
_____ 07224-9 **ENTWINED DESTINIES #136** Rachel Wayne $1.95
_____ 07225-7 **TEMPTATION'S KISS #137** Sandra Brown $1.95
_____ 07226-5 **SOUTHERN PLEASURES #138** Daisy Logan $1.95
_____ 07227-3 **FORBIDDEN MELODY #139** Nicola Andrews $1.95
_____ 07228-1 **INNOCENT SEDUCTION #140** Cally Hughes $1.95
_____ 07229-X **SEASON OF DESIRE #141** Jan Mathews $1.95
_____ 07230-3 **HEARTS DIVIDED #142** Francine Rivers $1.95
_____ 07231-1 **A SPLENDID OBSESSION #143** Francesca Sinclaire $1.95
_____ 07232-X **REACH FOR TOMORROW #144** Mary Haskell $1.95
_____ 07233-8 **CLAIMED BY RAPTURE #145** Marie Charles $1.95
_____ 07234-6 **A TASTE FOR LOVING #146** Frances Davies $1.95
_____ 07235-4 **PROUD POSSESSION #147** Jena Hunt $1.95
_____ 07236-2 **SILKEN TREMORS #148** Sybil LeGrand $1.95
_____ 07237-0 **A DARING PROPOSITION #149** Jeanne Grant $1.95
_____ 07238-9 **ISLAND FIRES #150** Jocelyn Day $1.95
_____ 07239-7 **MOONLIGHT ON THE BAY #151** Maggie Peck $1.95
_____ 07240-0 **ONCE MORE WITH FEELING #152** Melinda Harris $1.95
_____ 07241-9 **INTIMATE SCOUNDRELS #153** Cathy Thacker $1.95

All of the above titles are $1.75 per copy except where noted

WHAT READERS SAY ABOUT
SECOND CHANCE AT LOVE BOOKS